My name is Franklin. Emily chose it because it sounded dignified to her, though admittedly she sometimes called me Frankie or even Frankster, two names that aren't so dignified, but I didn't mind because I believe nicknames can be an expression of love. In my mind, I thought of her as Em. Her parents didn't call her that. Just me. No one else called me Frankie. Just Em.

"Franklin?" Chester says now. "I like that name. It suits you."

"I do, too. I'll probably never hear it from a person again, though."

Also by Cammie McGovern

Chester and Gus

Just My Luck

Frankie and Amelia

CAMMIE McGOVERN

HARPER

An Imprint of HarperCollinsPublishers

Library of Congress Control Number: 2021938318
ISBN 978-0-06-246333-3

Typography by Aurora Parlagreco
22 23 24 25 26 PC/CWR 10 9 8 7 6 5 4 3 2 1
❖
First paperback edition, 2022

For Tara Weikum and Margaret Riley King,
cat lovers both

CHAPTER ONE

I'M NOT SURE HOW LONG I'VE been sitting on the woodpile watching this boy through the window of his house. Maybe a day? Perhaps two? At first, I hardly noticed him because the outdoors is such a busy place and I have to keep myself on alert. Leaves blow, winds rustle, voles have litters of little blind babies that are easier for a larger-sized cat like me to catch.

I started watching the boy in the window on a sunny afternoon following a full meal from a tipped-over garbage can. Lying on the tarp-covered wood, still groggy, I suddenly felt a hair-raising prickle of danger. *Something's watching me*, I thought, and indeed, there he was. Standing in the window, staring out.

I crouched in a ready-to-spring position. A misjudgment on my part, I'll admit, considering he was about sixty yards away with a house and window between us.

I have to say, though, his gaze was so intense, I couldn't look away. I sat up on my perch and initiated a staring contest, an old game my mother used to play with neighborhood cats to establish territorial boundaries. *I've got my eye on you* is the message behind the game. *Not one paw on this side of the driveway.*

In a two-cat staring contest, the winner is the one so confident of victory he shuts his eyes and falls asleep first. A one-cat staring contest with some other creature has a different set of rules. This boy isn't staring at me in a territorial way. In fact, as I finally realize, he isn't staring at me *at all.* He's watching the same things I like to watch: the play of light through the leaves on the grass, a windblown leaf dancing across. His gaze is so intent I wonder for a second if he might *be* a cat, somehow disguised in a boy costume.

I drift off to sleep, which, if he is a cat, makes me the winner in this competition.

"Excuse me, but do you have a home of your own?"

This is unexpected. I'm being woken up by a brown dog on the ground, staring up at me. Of course I don't answer him.

"My name is Chester," he says. "I heard Sara and Marc talking inside. They're worried that you don't have a family or anywhere to live."

"Of course I have a family," I say, but I don't go into any details: I haven't seen them in a long time and I can't seem to find them.

I've never spoken with a dog before because my mother always told me not to. Dogs are the sworn enemy of cats. My mother taught me this when I was a kitten. The only animals we hate more than dogs are other cats, who, in addition to having staring contests, will pick a fight if you so much as walk a few feet into a territory they've decided is "theirs." Admittedly, I used to do this back when I had a home and it seemed important not to let any other cat near it. Now that I've been a wandering cat myself, I realize some of those old battles seem silly.

I look away from the dog and blink up into the sun. "Are you hungry?" the dog says. "Sara is inside looking for something you might like to eat. She's wondering if you like canned tuna fish."

Oh my. It's been weeks since I've had a meal of canned food, and yes, tuna fish has always been one of my favorites. If this is a guard dog, he's not doing a very good job of scaring me off.

"Here she comes!" he says. "She might tell you to eat slowly. That's what she says to me sometimes."

"Here you go, sweetheart," the woman says. She puts the bowl of food down at the other end of the woodpile, too high for the dog to reach, which is nice. I don't know if he would make a dive for it, but he might. "Dogs and cats will always fight," my mother used to say. "And cats will always win. It's sad, really. Dogs don't have claws and we do. You should always beware of dogs, but you should also feel a little sorry for them. Most of them don't care about anything except their people. It's embarrassing to watch, frankly—the way they follow commands and fetch balls. They've forgotten all their natural animal instincts."

Just as my mother once predicted, this dog doesn't realize we're supposed to be enemies and he doesn't make a move toward the tuna fish, which smells divine.

Instead he looks at me with his tongue hanging out in a friendly, dopey way. "Go on," he says. "It's okay. You don't have to be afraid of Sara. She's very nice."

I walk, tentatively, a little closer. I don't know how long it's been since I've had someone feed me. This whole time on my own, I've been trying to find my way back home to the family who opened such cans and offered them. I'm not sure why, but it's never occurred to me that other people might do the same. That if you lose track of one family, it might be possible to take up with another.

I move closer.

"Careful," the woman says. "Don't eat it too quickly. You might make yourself sick."

Behind me, the dog makes a happy, sneezy sound. "See, I told you she would say that!"

CHAPTER TWO

NATURALLY, I DON'T MAKE ANY RASH moves. Cats prefer to consider all their options unless their option is a vole scurrying across a lawn, and in that case, we'll move quickly. But choosing a new family is a commitment and requires some consideration.

On the one hand, this family has delicious cans of tuna fish. On the other hand, they also have a dog, which isn't a plus. However, this dog, Chester, doesn't seem to understand that he and I aren't meant to be friends.

He watched me the whole time I ate my lovely tuna meal and afterward he said, "If you don't have a family of your own right now, maybe you can come and live with us!"

I told him that was a ridiculous idea; I do have my own family. I just haven't seen them in a very long time. "It's a long story," I said. "I seem to be lost."

"Then you should live with us! We're a nice family!"

The other worry about choosing this family is that they seem to have a boy and no girls, and I'm used to girls. In my family there were two girls, but Emily was my favorite because she spent the most time thinking up games to play with me. Great games like dragging a piece of string around the house for me to chase and pounce on. I was a kitten back then, and up for playing with anything—clumps of feathers tied together with a rubber band, balls of aluminum foil. All of it seemed interesting and worth investing some time and energy in.

I don't know too many boys, but the ones I've met don't seem all that interested in making cat toys. They'd rather point sticks and fingers at things and pretend to shoot them. Emily had two boy cousins who once ate chicken wings at our house and used me as a napkin afterward to wipe their fingers off. It still makes me shudder to think about them.

That afternoon when Chester is out in the yard to pee, I tell him my hesitations about living in a house with a boy.

He listens and lifts his nose to the air. "I bet that chicken wing sauce tasted good, though."

"It did, but that's not the point. The point is, boys like to do things that cats aren't interested in. They bounce balls on driveways and aim toy guns at things, and cats don't like any of that."

"Gus isn't like that. He doesn't do any of those things."

So far I've watched Gus mostly stare at me out the window. I've also seen him bounce up and down when a bird flew into its nest on the porch. I have to admit, Gus does look a little different.

"Do his friends come over and crash little toy cars into each other?"

"No. Gus doesn't have any friends, though we're trying to work on that."

"What does he do?"

"He likes doing the same things you do. Staring out the window and watching birds. Things like that."

This is what I've seen him do and I have to admit: it sounds strange. Not for a cat, but for a boy.

"And sunlight? Does he like watching sunlight on blades of grass?"

"I don't know. He might. He doesn't talk a lot, so I have to go with my instincts sometimes, but my instinct is yes, he likes watching blades of grass."

I'm curious now. This is a family that serves tuna fish and has a cat-boy.

I'm moving closer to a decision.

CHAPTER THREE

"IT'S SO NICE TO HAVE YOU inside," Chester says. "I can take you for a tour if you'd like, or you can just walk around by yourself. Mostly I spend my days with Gus in his room or else on my bed here in the kitchen. Here's my food bowl and my favorite chew toy. What else can I show you? Maybe my water bowl?"

Clearly this dog has different priorities than I do. He's all about showing me objects lying around on the ground and I'm looking around for high places with enough space for me to lie down and get a look around. It's surprisingly unnerving being inside a house again after all this time outside. Every noise seems loud and echoes a little. I know ceilings don't usually fall down on cats, but I keep being startled and worrying that they might.

The hardest part is having everyone stare at me at once. I'm a beautiful cat, large for my species, with a lot of fluffy fur that's been hard to keep clean these last few weeks. I might have a few burrs stuck in my coat, but the way this mother and father are going on, you might think I was wearing a bag of trash on my back.

"First things first, we take him to the vet," Marc, the dad, says. "Then to a groomer. I don't know what they can do with that coat of his. They may have to shave the whole thing."

Shave it?! My glorious mane?

A few hours later as I frantically work to clean myself up, Chester tries to make me feel better. "Actually, going to the vet is much worse than going to the groomer."

As it turns out, he's right. The vet *is* much worse. He pulls me out of the terrible cage I've been locked in and, though he's got a long white beard and flyaway hair, he laughs like I'm the funny-looking one. "Yep. I'd say he's at least part Maine coon all right," he tells Sara, who has brought me. "You can tell by the ears and this big fluffy tail. Plus, of course, the size. He's almost twenty pounds even though you say he's been living on his own for a while. That's a Maine coon for you."

He laughs even more at this, though I can't see that he's said anything funny.

The vet keeps going. "People love these cats. They have a unique personality."

True.

"Very independent and resourceful."

Also true, I think, though I'm not 100 percent sure what that second word means. Then he adds something that is extremely interesting: I am the largest domestic cat breed in America.

I'll admit there have been times in the past few weeks on my own when I've been hurt by the things other cats have called me. Names like "Big Boy" and "Tugboat." I've never liked getting into the thick of it with these types of cats, or having to justify my long hair and fluff. I've learned from experience the name-callers never believe you anyway and too often the jokes only get worse when you mount a defense. That's when I have to turn sideways and puff myself up even more to show who really is the biggest of them all.

To tell the truth, though, I've never been quite sure where I fit in on the cat size continuum. Now I know. I am the biggest. Period. It almost makes me want to get back out there and find a few of the jesters from my past and pass along this information.

"Maine coons are also very people-focused. Almost like a dog."

People-focused? Almost like a dog? What is he *talking* about?

"There's an old legend that Maine coons descend from the royal cats who once belonged to the king and queen of France. Just before the French Revolution, when the monarchy was overthrown, their cats were sent to America, where the royal family planned to make their escape. The family didn't make it, so the cats were let loose to fend for themselves, which they've been doing very well ever since."

I like this story a lot and wouldn't mind hearing more, but apparently this vet is more interested in stabbing me with needles than he is in filling in a few details.

By comparison, the groomers aren't so bad. All they do is shave some pesky areas where I've had bits of tree bark and leaves stuck to me with pine sap for quite some time. I feel cleaner and fluffier than I have in a while.

When I get home, I share the vet's story with Chester. "Apparently I come from a long line of royal cats kept by kings and queens. Palace cats, we were called. Then something happened—I'm not sure what—but the kings and queens were killed and all their cats had to live out in the woods."

Chester cocks his head, the way dogs do sometimes. Like they're confused, or maybe they don't believe what you just said.

"If they were royal cats, how did they know what to eat in the woods?"

"Cats are smart that way. We figure things out." I don't want to brag too much, but I've just survived on my own for quite some time. "We don't just sit around and wait to get food put in our bowl at the same time every day. We keep up our hunting skills."

Chester lies down and puts his head on his paws. Maybe this was a mean thing to say. I suspect Chester isn't much of a hunter, but I'm not a good judge of other animals' feelings. The point is that this is a good story.

Emily loved having stories read to her and so did I. I'll admit I couldn't always follow the ones where witches put spells on girls and made them spin straw into gold, but I still liked the way things usually get very bad for a while in stories, and then it always works out in the end. I feel like my own story is playing out right now. Everything was great in the beginning, then it was very hard for a while, and now here I am.

CHAPTER FOUR

OF COURSE IT'S NOT THE END, though. Stories keep going.

So far, I've lived with this family for two days and I still haven't really met the boy I had the staring contest with. If I'm in a room, he usually turns around and walks out. I ask Chester if there's something different about him.

"Yes," Chester says. "He has autism. And seizures. That makes him a little different."

Because I don't know what those words mean, I walk away and pretend not to care.

After a while, though, I circle back because I'm curious, and Chester keeps going. "Autism means he doesn't talk very much or play like other boys. Seizures feel like lightning in his head and sometimes make him fall down. My job is to warn him when a seizure is coming and stay with him afterward."

Dogs and their "jobs." They all think they have one, which isn't true of course. Emily's neighbors had a dog who thought it was his job to greet his family with a shoe in his mouth every time they came home.

I remind Chester that I don't like boys very much. I tell him what my mother used to say: "Boys are unpredictable. They'll drop you into frightening water situations and when they're scolded, they'll tell their mothers, 'He really liked it. I swear!' Little girls aren't as bad. Sometimes they'll cradle you like a baby and feed you milk from a bottle, which might sound nice but just makes you dizzy."

"Gus doesn't do any of that," Chester says. "He's not like other boys. He also doesn't like sports or balls. He hates gym class at school. He used to hate a lot of things about school, but that's starting to change."

"How do you know all this?"

Chester brightens. "I go to school with him! I'm a seizure-response dog!"

Suddenly I realize: "Are you a *service dog*?"

"That's right! I wasn't official for a long time, but now I'm certified and everything." He's trying not to brag, I can tell, but it's hard for him to hide how proud he is of himself.

My mother warned me about service dogs. "Every animal instinct has been removed. They live for the sole purpose of serving a person. It's sad, really. You must never make fun of a service dog if you see one. It isn't nice."

I get the feeling that Chester doesn't think it's sad to serve a person—he's happy about it.

After three days I realize Chester is right. Gus isn't like any boy I've ever known before. He doesn't do karate kicks or movie imitations. He doesn't pull my tail or think I like it when he flattens my ears to make my eyes look big. He doesn't even look in my direction. In fact, he seems about as interested in Chester as he is in me, which is to say, not very. Poor Chester hovers near his knee, staring up, tail wagging hopefully, and Gus hardly notices him either. It's like he's staring at something else, but none of us can see it.

One morning, Gus does this for a long time, even though we're all staring at him.

"Gus?" his mom finally says. "Are you okay?"

He doesn't say anything.

"*Is* he okay?" I ask Chester, who ignores me. "He doesn't look okay."

Apparently Chester can't hear anything if he's staring at the boy.

"I have to keep my eye on him," he tells me later. "That's my job. I can't let myself get distracted."

"I like to watch faucets drip, but I don't call it a job," I point out.

"Faucets are different from people."

I roll my tail at that and walk away. Honestly. I know they're different; I'm making a point. *You have the same impact. A faucet doesn't care if you watch it or not.*

The whole morning is the same with Gus. His dad asks him questions and he doesn't answer. His mom touches his shoulder and he moves away. Chester doesn't touch him, but he's never more than a few inches away.

Eventually, the worried silence passes. Everyone stops staring at Gus and I have to admit—I've decided that Gus intrigues me a little. I like people who don't care what anyone thinks. He reminds me of me.

I want to let him know that I won't be pestering him the way others do. I brush myself around his ankles, the best way that I know of to communicate with a person. Usually I reserve it for food needs, but not always. In this case, for instance, my bowl is full. I'm trying to say something else: *I like you. You're okay. The others in this house, I'm not so sure about.*

WHAP!

17

He's kicked me! Across the room! There's a flurry—everyone descending on me at once. "Gus, no!" his mom says. "You must *never* kick an animal."

She picks me up and cuddles me, which is both awkward and a little nice. It's been a long time since anyone has scratched me behind my ears and I forgot how nice it can be.

The next time I see Gus, I keep my distance, a concept Chester will apparently never understand. He doesn't care if Gus looks at him or not; he sits beside him and stares at him the way I only stare at things I'm hoping to pounce on or eat. Chester isn't planning to eat Gus or anything interesting like that.

He's already told me: he's waiting for Gus to *need* him.

"Need you for *what*?" I asked.

"Different things. Sometimes I'll find a shoe if it's under the bed. Usually I help him manage his feelings. He gets overwhelmed easily. Touching me helps him cope—especially if we're at school—but he doesn't always remember that. I have to keep my eye on him so I'm there when he needs me."

I remember another thing my mother once said about dogs: "Some of them get so caught up in their humans' lives, they forget they're a dog. They talk about everything they do with their people—go to the beach, play Frisbee, watch TV. They have no *idea* how silly they sound."

I wonder if I should tell him, *You don't really go to school. You just pretend you do.*

And then I'm surprised.

Apparently he really *does* go to school. Or else he finds a very good hiding spot all day long. "Where *were* you?" I ask when I finally see him again, lying in his usual spot in the kitchen.

"I told you. School. I spend the day there with Gus."

I've never heard of such a thing. "Do cats go to school, too?"

"I don't think so. I've never seen one."

"Are there *a lot* of dogs?"

"I don't think so. I'm the only one I've ever seen."

Does this mean Chester isn't so dopey after all? Is it a school for children with very smart pets? I wouldn't mind applying if that's the case.

Of course not, though. I should have known. "I'm there to help Gus. I don't really follow what they're learning. Maybe a little bit here and there."

"If you go to school all day, you must know how to read."

"Not really. Maybe a few words."

If I ever went to school, I would definitely learn how to

read. I'm tired of lying on newspapers and only being able to look at the pictures. "Wouldn't you like to know what's going on in the world, Dopey?"

He gives me a sad look. "My name is Chester."

I feel bad. I usually don't say this name out loud; I just think it occasionally. I remember the other cats who have called me names. "You're right. I'm sorry."

To make him feel better, I surprise myself and tell him more of my own sad story than I've told anyone in a long time. "I used to have my own name. And my own family, too."

He looks up, surprised.

Gus's mom keeps talking about naming me, but then his dad makes terrible suggestions that I assume must be some kind of stab at humor because Sara laughs and usually says, "Seriously, we have to think of something."

So far, Marc's suggestions have been: Butterball, Captain Fluff, and Orson Welles, which I don't understand. Sara likes Puffinstuff, which also makes no sense.

My name is Franklin. Emily chose it because it sounded dignified to her, though admittedly she sometimes called me Frankie or even Frankster, two names that aren't so dignified, but I didn't mind because I believe nicknames can be an expression of love. In my mind, I thought of her as Em.

Her parents didn't call her that. Just me. No one else called me Frankie. Just Em.

"Franklin?" Chester says now. "I like that name. It suits you."

"I do, too. I'll probably never hear it from a person again, though."

He lies down and puts his chin on one paw. I'm right about this and there's not much he can say.

"What was your family like?" he finally asks. Everyone is asleep. We'd never have this conversation if the family was around. They take all his attention, even when they aren't asking anything of him.

"It's been a while since I've seen them." It's hard for me to talk about this without feeling as if I've got a hair ball in my throat. "I don't really remember too much."

He raises his eyebrows as if he knows this isn't true, which it isn't.

"Okay, fine. There were two sisters and some parents. Emily was the younger one. I was her favorite. She used to bring me slices of American cheese, which was the only food she could open herself. She was too young to work a can opener."

"That sounds nice. Was she your person?"

"What does that mean?"

"Did you go places and do activities together?"

"Not really. Activities involve car rides and cats don't like those."

"How about around the house? Did you play games inside?"

Just remembering the string that Emily used to drag around the house makes my throat close up again. "Sometimes," I say softly. "Like I said, it was a long time ago."

"Emily is a pretty name."

"I always thought so."

"Do you think she's still looking for you?"

It's a question I haven't let myself ask since that terrible time I watched them fill their car with the suitcases I'd just spent the night sleeping on top of. At first, I was sorry they were taking my perfectly proportioned bed; then it seemed they were taking more than that: coolers, bags of groceries, pillows, sleeping bags.

When I spotted the cat carrier, I started to panic and darted outside. I'd only ridden in a car a few times before, and after the last trip, when I lost half my weight in anxious fur shedding, I vowed to never do it again. I had to hide or else I'd get put in the car with everything else. Obviously, I wasn't thinking too clearly. Emily called for me and I hid myself deeper in the bushes. She started to cry, which

I didn't understand, so I shut my eyes. I don't like to watch emotions, especially when I'm feeling them myself.

"We'll have to go without him, sweetheart," Emily's mother said. "We have to get to the cabin before dark. He'll be okay. We'll leave food on the porch and have the neighbors check up on him. Cats are pretty amazing the way they can take care of themselves. You'll see. We'll be back in two weeks and he'll probably be on the porch waiting for us."

I came out of my hiding spot before they drove away, but it was too late. They were all in the car that was backing out of the driveway. No one was looking for me anymore.

They'll be gone for two weeks? I thought.

Genghis Khan ate most of the food they left out before I could even find it. When I did, it was two empty bowls with kibble crumbs at the bottom. I might have been the biggest cat in the neighborhood, but he was the scariest. With only half a tail and one ear chewed off, no cats I knew crossed paths with him.

"Looks like you'll be hunting for a while," he said as he walked away from my bowls. "Good luck with that."

I remembered being a kitten and watching my mother track a few voles in our yard, but I never saw her catch one. "We do it for fun," she explained after the third vole got away from her. "Canned food tastes better. These little ones

23

are all fur and bones. I prefer not to catch them. Chipmunks are harder to catch, especially when they disappear in the cracks of a stone wall. With them, it's a patience game. You sit and wait until they come out and they're a wonderful meal if you can get one. Plus their remains make a nice present for you to leave on the front porch. It's like Christmas for your family. They sweep it up and save it in a plastic bag. Just watch. It's very satisfying."

The whole first day after Emily's family left, I wandered around looking for chipmunks. I heard squeaks in the wall and under the house, but I never found one. When night came, I got so scared that I slept in the only safe spot I could find, on a shelf in the garden shed, above the lawn mower. I knew I'd wake up if another animal came in.

Technically, none did, but when it got really dark, I realized I wasn't alone. I heard movement above me. It wasn't one thing; it was many. Twitching and rocking and finally, *flying*. Mice that fly? My mother had never mentioned such a thing.

"Those are just bats," Genghis Khan told me the next day. He'd come back to check on my bowl, which of course was still empty. At first, I'd hid from him behind a pile of toys on the porch, then I couldn't believe it: he stretched out in a patch of sun, looked right over at me, and asked how I was doing. I was so surprised, I told him the truth—not very well. I said I hadn't eaten in a day and I'd hardly slept with all the noise in the garden shed.

"Bats are impossible to catch. Don't bother trying."

"Why do they go out at night?"

"They're blind, I guess, so it's all the same to them. They have pretty good ears so they listen for their food and catch it then. Less competition."

The next night, I stayed awake to watch how the bats did it. They were hunting for bugs, who apparently don't sleep either because they got plenty. When it was almost morning and the bats started coming back in the shed, I asked one of them, "Have you ever caught a chipmunk?"

"We're too little. We couldn't possibly."

"How little are you?" I asked. I hadn't eaten in two days. Maybe I should forget the chipmunk and settle on something smaller like one of these bats.

It was like the bats read my mind. That night, as I stared up at them, one called out, "We're all bones and wings. We taste terrible. Plus, we're too high for you to get."

I wasn't sure if he was just tricking me. That's what other animals did sometimes, my mother once warned us. They trick you into not eating them. It was a favorite tactic of mice, who all become great speech-makers while they die. They make declarations about their lives and why you shouldn't eat them. My mother said, "I always listen, but I also eat them anyway. You can't let other animals mislead you. They'll all try, and you have to follow your core instincts. We all have to survive and we must do what we have to."

I spent the rest of that night trying to catch a bat to eat and it turned out he was right, they were too high up.

CHAPTER FIVE

CHESTER MUST BE INTERESTED IN THIS story because he asks me about it the next night after Gus is asleep. "What happened after you figured out you couldn't eat the bats?" he says like he's been thinking about it for a while and it's been worrying him.

I keep going with my story. I tell him that I followed the bats outside and practiced hunting with my ears, which wasn't as hard as I'd thought it would be. I also figured out I could see much better than expected. And there were lots of other animals out at night. On my first evening foray, I met a raccoon named Rocky who taught me about eating compost. Watermelon rinds were his favorite, but not mine. When I pointed out that there were worms in his food, he said he ate those, too, no problem.

"I guess I like my food a little fresher," I said, watching him brush some dirt from a dried orange peel.

"You want fresh, then you'll have to come with me for some trash-can tipping. We'll have to travel, though. This neighborhood all has locks on their cans, but a few blocks over, you won't believe what you can find. Steaks, chicken patties, empty tuna cans . . ."

I was scared to leave our block, but I was so hungry I knew I had to try.

"Tuna fish cans?" I said.

"Lots of them." Rocky nodded. "In open boxes. You don't even have to tip them. You just reach in and help yourself. Me, I'm not crazy about empty cans. You might be different."

My first night traveling with Rocky, I ate better than I had in ages, though it took a while to find what I wanted. He clawed items out of the garbage bag and held them up in the streetlight to see if I was interested. "Bread? Corn cobs? Onion skins?"

He dipped each bite in a puddle of water before tasting. "Ah, lovely," he'd say.

I licked at the items he laid down on the ground for me, thinking maybe the water had been an effort to wash my food before offering it, which was nice. I was starving, but nothing tasted like food to me, until he yanked out a chicken carcass, drippy with grease and bits of meat. My heart leapt. I reached for it.

"Wait! A dip first," he said, holding it over the puddle.

"No!" I cried. Was he really going to wash away all the delicious juice? He stopped and looked at me. "I mean, no thank you."

He shrugged and tossed the whole thing to me. "I'm not a big one for chicken bones anyway," he sighed.

I ate for hours that night and slept the whole next day in my shed hiding spot. The neighbors came by and left food for me, which I didn't know until Genghis told me that a few skunks came along and helped themselves.

It had only been four days and I already felt like a different cat. I became a night prowler and, as often as I could, followed Rocky wherever he went. He had a better sense of direction than I did. Every night he walked me back to my yard. By that point, I liked him so much that I tried to walk like him, with a side-to-side waddle, stopping every few feet to stand up and listen.

When I asked what he was listening for, he said, "Cars, mostly. Cars are our number one enemy."

I thought about the car that had taken my family away. I agreed.

"They come out of nowhere. They don't see at night like we do and they don't stop." He shook his head sadly. "I don't understand them. They don't even eat what they kill, they just leave it behind on the side of the road. Do you understand that?"

I didn't.

For all his caution, I noticed Rocky took some surprising chances. Sometimes in our wanderings, he walked down the middle of the road, not to the side, where he could duck into bushes like I did. "I like these white lines," he told me. "They help me see where I'm going."

"But isn't it dangerous?" I asked from the side.

"Not for me. That's why I'm always listening."

Two nights later, we walked even farther than usual. The road was deserted. From his spot in the middle, he told me more about his life. He said raccoons like socializing but can never figure out how to get along with each other. "We always fight. I don't know why that is."

"You've been so nice to me."

"Exactly. If you were a raccoon, I wouldn't be. I don't know why—it's just not in my nature. If you were a raccoon, I'd fight you for every scrap of food we found. With you, it's different, Franklin. I kind of like helping you. I don't know why. It's strange."

We had a glorious time that night, stumbling into a sub-division he'd never found before where some trash barrels didn't even have lids.

"It's like they laid out a buffet!" he exclaimed.

I didn't know what a buffet was, but there sure was a lot of good food, some of it still warm. We'd already been through three trash cans when we found the salmon.

"Oh my goodness," he said after he tore a hole in the bag and peeked inside. "This is our lucky night, Franklin!"

That was my first time trying real salmon, which is different and much better than cat food salmon. It was Rocky's favorite, too, and it was nice of him to share. He could eat a lot more than I could, which might have explained what happened later.

I ate my fill and he ate the rest, sucking juices off his paws. When we finally finished and started back home, he moved slowly and groaned a little. "My stomach is dragging on the ground. I'm afraid it's slowing me down a bit." He stopped to rest on his painted line in the road. "Boy oh boy, I wish I'd been smart like you and stopped eating when I was full!"

It was the first time anyone had ever called me smart. Lately, I just thought of myself as hungry and scared. The compliment made me feel good. Maybe I was more like Genghis Khan than I thought. A survivor—scrappy and smart. Not the cat I'd been earlier, curled on a shelf behind a lawn mower, scared of bats and anything else that moved.

Rocky began licking his paws again, and I worried that he might be settling down for a nap in the middle of the road. "We should keep walking," I said. "We still have a pretty long way to go."

"Sure." He yawned. "It's hard, though, isn't it? Walking after a big meal."

"A little. But I don't know my way home and I need to get back."

"Sure, sure. We'll keep going." He didn't move. "Problem is, I think I might have eaten some plastic bag. Those never sit well with me."

All of a sudden, it was like he started to glow. He sat up on his hind legs and got even brighter. When I finally realized what was happening, it was too late. A car came up over the hill and tried to swerve, like its front tires didn't want to hit him, but its back tires didn't care.

It was the worst thing I've ever seen. I try to forget it, but sometimes I dream about it and it's like it's happening all over again.

I tried to stay with him as long as I could, even though he was already gone. As the sun rose, a truck pulled up and stopped on the side of the road, near the bush I was hiding under. A man got out. It took him less than a minute to scoop Rocky into a black plastic bag. I hoped the man would eat him so his death would be useful to someone. I feared he wouldn't, though. I hadn't heard people talk a lot about eating raccoons.

After he drove away, I looked around. I knew I was nowhere near my house. Here, the cars drove faster and the houses were closer together. No one had sheds where a lost cat could hide for a day.

I learned a lot from my week with Rocky, but I learned even more that first week without him. For instance, I learned that there were other cats like me prowling around and none of them wanted to be my friend. Quite the opposite, in fact. They had only to catch a whiff of me and they were hissing and rattling threats from their throats. I'd been through this before with Genghis Khan, but we were old enemies, which made us almost friends compared to these cats. Genghis and I would do our favorite tricks—turn sideways, fluff up, hiss a bit—if we crossed paths unexpectedly. But we were never mean. We didn't call each other cruel names like these cats were quick to do, insinuating that I had become a plus-sized cat. It was true that eating with Rocky had added a bit of girth to my middle. Walking like a raccoon had accommodated that.

The cat antagonism only got worse. Ignoring them didn't work. Neither did walking sideways to show them how big I really was. To them, it was an invitation to go ahead, jump on me, and bite my ears while they were at it.

Pretty soon I was hiding out during the day and only prowling for food at night. It turns out cats aren't as good at tipping trash cans or opening plastic bags as raccoons are, which was terrible to realize until I remembered that I was a much better hunter than Rocky. The first night that I caught a mouse was a turning point. The mouse got chatty before the end and I remembered my mother's words. Let them talk for a while, then eat them anyway.

CHAPTER SIX

I'VE TOLD THIS STORY OVER THE course of several nights. For the first time, though, Chester looks shocked. "You *killed* the mouse?"

"Yes. I think that's nicer than eating it alive, don't you?"

"I could never kill another animal. Ever."

I can't tell if he's serious. "Not even if you're hungry?"

"If I'm hungry, I go to my food bowl and sit near it and wait. That usually works."

"But let's just say your people haven't been home for a long time. Maybe they went away and forgot all about you."

He considers this. "That would never happen."

"Anything can happen, Chester. Believe me. You can't put all your faith in people. An animal has to be able to take care of himself."

He doesn't like hearing this. He keeps looking at the door like he's hoping someone will come home and we can stop talking. After a long silence, he says quietly, "I can take care of myself. I eat flies sometimes."

Just then the door *does* open and I'm relieved, too. Now I don't have to tell poor Chester that tiny bats might live on bugs, but big dogs can't. Or not for long, anyway. It's Gus's dad, who's come home with something in a big, flat box that smells delicious.

"No cats on counters," he says when I jump up to have a closer sniff. He pushes me off and sneezes.

One thing about Marc is he sneezes a lot. He also blows his nose with loud, honking sounds that are, frankly, unpleasant to be around.

Sara and Gus come home a little later. Marc is still sneezing and honking. Sara says, "Oh, Marc, are the pills still not working?"

"I don't think there's a lot they can do when a cat has this much fur and leaves some behind everywhere he goes. I thought the grooming would help, but this is bad, Sara."

I don't understand. What does my fur have to do with pills and sneezing?

"They've worked when you're around other cats."

"Right. But I have to say—" SNEEZE. "I don't think—"

36

SNEEZE. "I can keep living with this one."

Gus laughs and hops up and down every time his dad sneezes. He thinks it's funny, but I don't.

Suddenly I realize: they think that *I'm* the reason Marc is sneezing so much and blowing his nose all the time. Never in my life have I told anyone to sneeze and blow their nose. If anything, I find it unpleasant and I'd encourage him *not* to do it while I'm around. Once, I actually felt the mist from his sneeze land on my fur. I had to bathe myself for hours afterward.

For the rest of the evening, I stay curled up in the corner and pretend to sleep, but really, I'm listening to everything they say.

It's not good.

Apparently the problem is something called allergies. Marc's allergies mean I can't live here anymore even though I've gone to the doctor and had my shots and gotten used to everyone, including Chester.

This is what Sara says: "Puffinstuff can't stay here, I'm afraid. It's just not working."

I hear this and walk away with a funny squeezing in my chest. When I first spotted Gus and talked to Chester about the possibility of taking up with this family, I assumed it was mostly a food-based decision. Families are fine, but I'd had one once and I didn't need to get attached like that again. Better not to, I reasoned.

Now, I have to admit—spending all this time watching Chester watch Gus has gotten me interested in other things about them. I don't mind hearing Chester tell me about Gus's day at school. I like Sara's stories about what happened at pickup. I especially like a new ritual Sara has started after Gus goes to sleep where she comes downstairs for a glass of water and pulls me into her lap for a chin rub. Every night, she tells me I'm doing a mighty fine job being a cat, which is a nice thing to hear when you spend all day with a dog who likes to talk about his work.

For the first time, I don't mind this terrible name that Sara has chosen for me. In fact, I'd happily keep the name if they'd let me stay.

"What should we do?" Sara says later that night when she and Marc have both come down for water. "It's not easy to find a home for a full-grown cat."

I open one eye and see Sara stare down at me. She has a funny look on her face. I can't tell what it means. I wish I could go over and ask Chester, but I'm afraid if I walk across the room, someone will pick me up and put me outside. This is the worst part about living with people. Someone is always picking you up and putting you wherever they want.

If I was better at reading people's expressions, I might be able to guess what Sara is thinking, but I'm not. Sometimes Sara purses her lips the way she did after the vet visit when she took me out of the carrier and held me for a while, saying my life has probably been so hard. I thought that meant she felt sorry for me and would let me do whatever I want, but apparently it meant she would brush my fur and apply an ointment that smelled terrible.

Now I look at her face—her lips folded into a thin line—and wonder if it means something even worse. "Oh, it breaks my heart," she says. "But we can't keep him, can we?"

"No," Marc says. "We can't."

They all look over at me. I close my eyes and pretend to sleep even though my heart is beating like crazy. I don't want to live on my own again. I like having friends like Chester to talk to and people like Sara to give me chin rubs. Telling Chester my whole story has reminded me of how hard it all was. I tried to make it sound exciting and even a little glamorous, but the main thing I remember is how scared I was most of the time. And lonely. After Rocky died, I never made another friend. I pretended I didn't care, especially after I had a terrifying brush with a fox and a bear in a single night, but I *did* care. I wanted to find another friend like Rocky, and I never did.

"Some animals aren't good at making friends," Rocky once told me. "Raccoons, we're too self-absorbed. We think about food more than we think about friends. The thing I've learned, though, is that it's nicer eating with someone else. Especially if the other animal doesn't eat a whole lot, like you for instance. You're a nice, light eater. I like that."

Here's what I really learned on my own: getting food is hard, but making friends is harder.

CHAPTER SEVEN

THE NEXT DAY, CHESTER TRIES TO explain what Sara is thinking. "Sara really likes you, but she has to think about her whole family. She and Marc spend most of their time worrying about Gus. That's their job, which I understand because it's my job, too."

Get Chester started and he'll go on all day about his service dog duties.

I don't care about that; I want to know how he knows what they're *feeling*. He can always tell. I can't. Sometimes I think everything seems fine and then Sara starts crying. Or the other way around: she seems mad and then she starts laughing. Chester isn't surprised but I always am.

"I can just tell," he says. "I mean, look at them. Can't you tell?"

When he says this, I look at them, sitting in the other room, watching TV. No, I can't tell.

"They're watching a scary movie. That's why their eyes are wide."

Their eyes didn't look wide to me. They looked the same. "What does that mean?"

He gives me a funny look, like it should be obvious. "They're *scared*."

They might be scaring themselves with movies, but I'm feeling scared with thoughts that I won't be able to live here much longer. Later that day, I try an experiment where I don't move from the spot I've been curled in. Maybe if I never move again, I'll never leave fur anywhere, and Gus's dad will stop sneezing and I won't have to leave.

It's not a great plan—I'll probably get hungry at some point, for instance—but at least I'll be safe and be able to stay.

I shut my eyes and pretend to sleep more. It's not long before I feel Chester breathing over me. I open one eye. "What is it?" I snap.

"Are you okay? You haven't moved for a long time."

"I'm fine. I've got a plan."

"What is it?"

"I'm going to stay right here and hopefully they'll stop

noticing me and forget all about throwing me out."

Chester cocks his head to one side. Admittedly, now that I've said it out loud, it doesn't sound like a great plan. What will I do when I get hungry? Chester would probably bring me food if I asked, but it's a lot to ask, especially if I like eating six or seven times a day.

"Okay," he says, and sits down. "Usually they remember and notice their pets, though. That's my experience."

"Well, I don't *have* another plan! That's it! I guess it's back to living in the wild and eating mice for me! I hope that doesn't upset you too much."

"It sounds sad. For the mice and for you. I have another idea, but I'll need to work on it before I tell you. I'm pretty good at ideas, but getting people to go along with them is harder. You have to get them to understand what you're saying and most of the time, they don't."

"What's your idea?"

"I'm not going to tell you. But I'm going to see if Gus can help."

I hate to say it, but that doesn't sound too promising. I've never seen Gus answer a question or seem like he's listening when someone talks to him. He makes funny sounds and bounces on his toes. Even though I like him because he likes watching birds through a window just like I do, I don't think he's going to be able to help me.

The next morning Chester is sitting in the kitchen, awake long before I am, wearing his silly-looking blue vest and looking excited.

"Morning, Franklin! The weekend's over! It's a school day again! Finally! I thought it would never come."

"Is going to school really this exciting for you?"

"Oh, sure! It's my job! Plus I have another job now, which is helping you! That'll make things more interesting. I feel pretty hopeful about this one."

I've already given up on the idea of staying in one place. The main problem is that you forget you made the plan and get up and move for no reason other than you saw a nice piece of paper on the floor that looked appealing for lying on. The next thing you know, Sara's rousing you out of a sound sleep, lifting you up, and saying, "Here's the article I've been looking for. Silly cat. Don't start lying all over Marc's work, now."

I'm my own worst enemy. I want to be invisible and instead I make myself a target.

I spend the rest of the day in the basement, wondering what Chester's plan might be. Is he finding me a job at school where I'd have to wear a vest and look silly, too? It's hard to imagine. Vests must get itchy and drive you crazy after a few minutes. Chester doesn't seem to mind his, but he doesn't have the same sensitive fur that I do.

Upstairs, I hear Sara on the phone.

"He's a *very* sweet cat. The vet said he might be part Maine coon." I rouse from my perch to start up the stairs and listen. "No, that's all right, Wendy, I understand. Of course you've got your hands full. We're just looking for a nice home and I remember how much you love animals."

I stop on the stairs as I hear her dial another number. "Ginny? It's Sara. Listen, this might seem out of the blue, but I remember your kids stopping in our yard to admire our cat the other day. That's right. Puffinstuff."

Oh, that name! I'll never land anywhere with a name like that, I fear. Then I remember the children she's talking about. One of them petted me with the toe of her shoe. My whiskers buzz in fear until I hear, "No, of course I understand. I know a pet is a big commitment."

It keeps going like this for a while. She calls more people and changes her strategy a little. "Cats really aren't all that much work, Bob. Some people say they take care of themselves. They go away and leave theirs alone all weekend."

Though I can't hear the other end of the conversation,

one by one they must say no, because Sara keeps saying, "No, I understand. I'll keep trying."

Finally she calls a name I recognize. The vet. "Dr. Terrine? We need to ask for your help." She tells him about trying to find my old family, about posting my picture on a "Missing Pets" website and getting no responses. "Now we're at a loss. I've spoken to the shelter and they've said they can keep him for a month, but if they can't find a home for him—well, you know what they'll do. They say with a big cat like him, fully grown, he has about a fifty-fifty chance. I just can't do that, Doctor, but I've been making calls all morning and I can't find anyone who will take him."

A fifty-fifty chance of *what*?

Chester is at school right now, but I wish he was here. He'd be able to explain all this.

A few hours later, I don't need Chester to explain anything because Sara just says it to Marc: "If I take him to a shelter, he'll die. Nobody will want him and in thirty days, they'll put him to sleep. We both know that."

Chester is lying behind me on his dog bed with his vest off. When he got home from school, he didn't say anything about his idea for me. Maybe he forgot. Apparently it was also chicken nugget day in the school cafeteria, which must have been a distraction, because that was all he said about his day. Why worry about my life when chicken nuggets are being dropped on the ground?

"Did you *hear* that, Chester? They're trying to kill me, I guess."

"No, Franklin. They're trying *not* to kill you. That's why she was crying. She doesn't want you to die."

She was *crying*? To be honest, it's hard for me to tell the difference between crying and needing to blow your nose.

"She's very upset about all this. She really likes you."

"How do you know that?"

"The way she looks at you when you walk around. It's very loving. I was actually jealous for a while. I don't think she ever looks at me that way, but maybe I just don't see it."

Jealous? "Why would a dog with his own bed and job and vest be jealous of a cat?"

"Sara *admires* you," Chester says. "I think maybe she wishes she could be more like you. Self-sufficient and independent. She likes those qualities."

Part of me wonders if this dog has been watching too much TV and part of me wishes I could see the world the way he does, where people make sense and everything they do can be explained. Being around Chester does make me feel better, though, I have to admit.

"What about your idea? Did you have any luck?"

He lies down on his bed and sets his head between his paws. "I'm still working on it. Gus has a friend he's been getting to know at school. Her name is Amelia and he thinks she only comes over to him because she loves me, but that's not true. She likes Gus, too. She loves all animals, but her favorites are cats; she talks about them all the time. She wants one of her own but her mother doesn't think she can handle the responsibility. She gets a little emotional sometimes. She's very smart at school things, but that doesn't always help her. Once she told me she's the best student in the whole grade at math, but she hates math."

"I'm sorry, Chester, but what does all this have to do with me?"

"I think you should go live with her. Then Gus and I could come visit you at her house and he could get to know her better."

He says this like it should have been obvious. To me, it wasn't obvious. "Oh. Did you ask her?"

"I can't ask her, obviously, but I'm trying to get Gus to."

I see the problem now. Gus never asks anyone a question. I've also never heard him answer a question. When he talks, it's usually in a room by himself to no one in particular. I once tried listening and I couldn't follow. He sang a few lines from a song and then told himself to always flush after he went to the bathroom. Except he wasn't in the bathroom. Since then I've noticed that he likes to remind himself of rules and then sings songs to make himself feel better about all these rules. I don't think he likes rules, but his brain can't help going over them.

I don't understand Gus.

I'm pretty sure I'm not alone. Sometimes his mom will come into the room, listen for a while, and say, "Gosh, Gus, I wish I could figure out what you're talking about. It sounds pretty interesting."

Then she leaves the room because she knows he won't explain it to her.

"That doesn't seem like a great plan to me," I tell Chester. "Gus's mom is pretty good at talking to other people and she couldn't get anyone to say yes. How is Gus going to get this girl to take me home?"

"She has to meet you first. We're doing a project at school where every kid practices public speaking by bringing something from home and telling a story about it. I think Gus should bring you!"

"To school?"

"Sure. It's a little scary at first, but you'll get used to it."

"Will I have to wear a vest? Because cats don't look good in vests. They don't fit us right."

"Oh, no. Only service animals have vests. They'd probably bring you in your carrier and leave you in it for most of the time. That way the children can look at you but you won't have to worry about anyone pulling your tail. At the end of the presentation, they'll take you out so the children can pet you and that's when Amelia will fall in love with you!"

Hmm. I don't love the idea of traveling in that terrible cage again. And tail-pulling children doesn't sound very appealing either. But of course, I *do* like the idea of a little girl falling in love with me again. I've never forgotten how that feels.

"Okay, Chester. It's not a bad idea, but how do we make it happen?"

"I'm trying to get Sara to think of the idea herself, but so far, it's not working."

"How do you do that?"

"I sit near her, and hope she can hear what I'm thinking."

"People can hear our thoughts?"

"Some people can. Gus hears mine. Not all the time, though. He has to be in the mood."

"How often is that?"

"Not very often. Lately, less and less. But I think that's because he's noticed Amelia and would like to be friends with her. He never hears what I'm thinking when she's around. He's too busy trying to think of something to say to her."

"Has he ever talked to her?"

"Not yet. But he will."

"Does he talk to other people at school?"

"Not really."

"So how would he do a speech or tell people a story about me?"

"If he writes it out ahead of time, he can use his talking computer. And maybe he could read some of it out loud. I've seen him do that before."

"In front of other people?"

"No." He looks down sadly. "Not in front of other people. But when we're alone in his room, he sometimes reads out loud."

I have to admit, I'm surprised to hear that Gus can read at all. Admittedly, I haven't thought a great deal about Gus. "Does Gus really understand what you're thinking?"

"Oh yes."

"Do you understand him?"

"Not all the time, but if we need to, yes. We understand each other."

CHAPTER EIGHT

CHESTER IS RIGHT! HE *CAN* GET people to read his thoughts! Or else he's just a very lucky dog. I almost fall off the sofa back I'm sleeping on when I hear Sara tell Marc she has a crazy idea for what to do with me. "We've been trying to think of a topic for Gus to deliver his speech on—what if we brought in Puffinstuff? We tell his whole story about how we found him and how much we love him and how sad we are that we can't keep him because of your allergies."

I'm not pretending to sleep anymore. My eyes are open, watching Marc's reaction.

Finally Marc says, "Do you think that's what Gus wants to do for his speech?"

"I don't know. Maybe! He hasn't said no when I've suggested it."

"Has he even *noticed* the cat?"

"Of course he has, Marc. Gus is the reason I saw him on the woodpile. He was looking in a different direction out the window. I was trying to figure out what had caught Gus's attention and there he was—a little pair of eyes staring back. That's what I want to tell the kids—that Gus notices and sees things other people don't. He's the one who first found Puffinstuff!"

She's right about this. Gus is the first person I noticed in this house and he's the first person who noticed me. Even though we still keep our distance these days, I think we still enjoy watching each other.

"Okay, then," Marc says. "Especially since we don't have any other ideas. And you're going to bring the cat in?"

"We'll keep him in the carrier the whole time unless there's someone who definitely thinks they might be able to bring him home and then we'll let that child meet him."

Chester is extremely pleased with himself when we talk that night after everyone has gone to bed. "I told you this would work! Don't look so worried."

"How do you know I'm worried?"

"You always clean yourself when you're worried, even if you've already had a few baths today."

I stop what I'm doing. It's unsettling to think that a dog

knows me this well. I lick my lips to get the fur off my tongue. Never mind this bath, I guess.

Finally I say this: "I don't know what to expect. I'm a cat who likes to keep his dignity. It's always a little daunting to go into unknown situations, that's all."

"I can see that."

"The last two times I went in a cat carrier anywhere was to the vet's office and the groomer, and that was highly unpleasant, as you remember."

"Oh sure."

"So I'll try to stay calm, but I can't promise anything."

"That's fine. I'll be there the whole time, Franklin. I won't let anything bad happen."

CHAPTER NINE

I DON'T KNOW WHY CHESTER BOTHERED promising something he can't deliver on.

Just as I feared, children are loud. Much louder than I expected. The inside of my box echoes with the screams and the thunderous sound of footsteps. I'd like to bury myself in the ratty old towel Sara's thrown in here, but it's scrunched in a corner, doing no good at all. I'm so dizzy, I can feel my fur flying from my body and sticking to the walls of this box. Soon it will be a fur-lined cave and I'll be bald.

Every once in a while I catch a glimpse of Chester, trotting calmly beside Gus. Easy for him to look okay; he's not riding in a ship through a storm that hits a rock every third step. I'm finally set down in what must be a classroom, but who knows—everything is too brightly lit for me to look around. The noise only grows louder. It crawls in my ears and twists my insides.

Footsteps, door slams, screaming voices.

I don't know if my claws will ever retract.

This is worse than the vet's office. Much worse.

Finally there's some reprieve. One voice hushes the others. "Look, everyone, we have a special treat today, but this treat can't stay for very long, so instead of starting with our morning meeting, we're going to start with our first speech of the day—from Gus!"

A merciful break from a teacher I can't see. I meow my thanks.

"Let's give Gus all our attention and listen with our whole bodies. He's written out his speech ahead of time and he's going to use his computer to help him deliver it. Remember, good listening, everyone!"

I guess it takes a long time for kids to sit down and stop talking because Gus doesn't start for a while. I've only heard him use his computer voice a few times. To me, it sounds jarring and strange, but that might be because my nerves are already jangled.

"Hello, everyone. I'd like you to meet Puffinstuff. He's a remarkable cat for many reasons. He's bigger and heavier than an average cat. He weighs more than twenty pounds, which is a lot for a cat. He might be part Maine coon, a breed that is rumored to descend from French royal cats."

I'm surprised. If I close my eyes, I don't mind listening to this speech. I like that he's called me remarkable. I also like the part about French royalty. This voice doesn't sound like how I imagine Gus thinks, but that's all right. Sara probably typed the words and Gus might have thought them.

Then he gets to the sad part of my story. I know that because his computer says, "Here's the sad part of my cat's story."

Some of the kids make noises like they don't want to hear anything sad. The teacher stands up and Gus stops his computer so she can talk. "Remember, everyone—we're listening right now. Amelia, no questions or comments until the end. After he's done, Gus will call on you and you'll be able to say whatever you'd like—within reason—okay?"

I twist around, only to realize I'll never be able to see Amelia's face from my windowless cave. Wherever she is, Amelia sighs in protest.

"Thank you for your patience, Amelia," the teacher says. "Okay, Gus. Keep going."

It's quiet for a while. I hear someone pressing buttons, but nothing comes out.

"Do you need help, Gus?" Sara says. She sounds worried.

This was going so well, and now it's not.

More silence. More buttons. Nothing.

"What could this be? We checked the batteries. It's right here on the screen."

I hear Chester say, *You could just read it, Gus.* The others don't hear him, of course, but I can. The question is: Can Gus hear him?

I don't hear an answer. Sara keeps working with the computer and telling the teacher she's sorry about the delay.

You don't have to be nervous, Chester says. *You're a very good reader.*

We all wait some more. Some of my fur drifts through the metal bars of my cage.

Everyone goes very quiet. I can't see what Gus is doing because my cage is in front of him, but the next thing I hear is his lovely, soft voice—much nicer than the computer voice.

"The sad part about my cat's story is that he can't live with us." His voice is slow. Chester is right—he likes to read carefully. "My father is allergic and the cat makes him sneeze. We have to find a new home for this wonderful, fluffy cat. If anyone thinks they might like this cat for their own or know of a good home for him, raise your hand. Thank you."

I can only see the four children right in front of me and none of them raise their hands.

Then I wonder if maybe the building is falling down because there's a huge noise. A rumbling like thunder, except it's not—it's children clapping.

They loved hearing your voice, Gus! Chester says. *That's why they're clapping.*

Now it's so loud I don't know if Gus can hear Chester. He lets out a high-pitched squeal that sounds like he's trying to block it all out. It's a good idea; I try it, too. When the kids stop clapping, only Gus and I are making our sounds. It's hard to stop or hear anything else.

Sara picks up my box and opens the door to put her hand in. "Shh, kitty. Shhh."

My heart is racing. I can't stop making noise.

"Do you want to come out now and let a few kids pet you?"

I don't know what I want. I'm a wreck.

"I'll hold you, sweetheart. It'll be okay."

I'm scared of the bright lights and all the noise that I know can start up again any minute. She pulls me out and I do the only thing I can think of: dig my claws into her shirt and climb up to her shoulder. But there's no relief there, just a more precarious spot where I can still see children circling around and pressing their hands toward me.

If all of them touch me, I'll never be able to get myself clean. I dig my claws in and Sara squeezes me hard. "No, Puff! That hurts!"

I don't care anymore. I have to get out of here, but anywhere I jump, I'll land on a child. A flash of brown moves under me.

I look away and then back. In my panic, I've forgotten about Chester. He sits down behind Sara where I can see him. He's ridiculously calm. "This is Amelia, Franklin. The girl I was telling you about."

There are five girls—maybe more—holding out their hands and pressing closer. "Which one?" I snarl.

"The one with the curly hair."

This helps a little, except not really, because she's standing behind Chester, away from the crowd. "Tell her to come over here and get me, for heaven's sake!"

"I can't. She doesn't understand me. Plus, she doesn't like crowds or being touched."

I can certainly relate to that.

"She also doesn't like these girls very much. She used to be friends with them, but she's not anymore."

Amelia's hair is curly like Emily's hair was. "Can you tell

her I'll go home with her if she'll get me off this shoulder?"

"No. She won't hear me."

Around us, the children's voices rise up: "I want him!" "I said it first! He's going home with me!"

"He can't go home with anyone until you ask your folks and I talk to them on the phone," Sara says. "I'm glad you're all interested, though. He's a wonderful cat. He's a little scared right now, but maybe we'll put him back in his carrier and he'll feel safer in there."

I panic all over. *Not the carrier!* I think.

Chester tries to help by nudging Sara as she pulls me off her shoulder. "Not now, Ches. I need to take care of the cat."

I try to look Amelia in the eye, which is hard for me. Maybe it's hard for her, too, because every time I look at her, she's looking away.

"Do something, Franklin!" Chester says. "Don't let her put you in the cage before you meet Amelia!"

I do whatever I can. I claw at Sara's shirt. I wriggle and squirm. I meow like crazy. Behind me, I hear a boy say, "Never mind, I don't want that cat."

I stiffen my legs and hiss.

Another girl says, "Me neither."

"Come on, Puff. You're not doing yourself any favors," Sara says firmly. "We're trying to make friends, not scare them away."

In spite of all my best efforts, I don't succeed. Sara jams me in the carrier and slams the door shut. "There! Safe and sound!" She tries to laugh, like we've been playing a game. "I promise you guys this is a sweet kitty. Do you have any questions about him? Yes, Emma?"

"Does he hunt other animals like mice and kill them?"

Yes, of course is the answer, but it's not what Sara says. "Not that we've ever seen."

"Does he get along with other animals?"

"At first he didn't, but now it seems like he loves our dog. We think he sees Chester like a dad or a big brother. He follows him around the house."

Well, this is embarrassing. I'll certainly never do that again.

"What's his name?"

I hold my breath. If anything's going to kill my chances for a new home, it'll be Sara telling these kids the dumb name she's given me.

For a long time, she doesn't answer. "Here's the thing," she finally says. "We don't really know his name. When we found him, he was a cat who'd obviously had a home and a family and a name once."

Just hearing her say this gives me hair balls in my throat again.

"Since we didn't know what it was, we called him our own name, but I think whoever takes him home can come up with their own name so he really feels like your cat."

This is nice. She knows her name is embarrassing and terrible. She's not going to saddle me with it forever. I feel bad now for all the clawing I did on her shoulders.

Everyone has ideas for new names.

"I'd name him Dr. Who."

"I'd name him Flash. Or Captain Marvel."

"I'd name him—"

I can only see Amelia out of the corner of my cage door. She's moved a little bit closer, but she still won't look at me. The other girls are losing interest, which helps. Amelia doesn't seem as scared of the boys. As she looks down, all I can see is her hair, which is puffy. I would like to pat it with a paw.

From what I can see, Chester is right. This girl is a loner like me and we'd make a good match. She doesn't put her finger through the bars on my door and poke at me, the way the other kids do.

She doesn't know what to say, though, and neither do I.

This is awkward.

It seems like maybe some of the other, louder kids will ask their parents first and will get me instead. Maybe she doesn't know how to ask her parents for things she really wants. Just like I have a hard time admitting certain things, like living on my own was lonely and I'd like to have a family again.

Cats don't like to admit those things. I worry Amelia might be the same way. Or maybe she's like Gus and doesn't talk very much.

That would be okay, I think.

Chester loves Gus, who never talks to him and seems like he ignores him, except now I know he doesn't because he followed Chester's suggestion and read his speech out loud. Some kids don't talk, but that doesn't mean they don't love their pets and listen to them when it matters.

Then I can't believe it—Amelia leans so close to my carrier, her lips press against the bars of my cage. I can smell what she had for breakfast—cereal and milk.

"Look, you guys! She's kissing the cat cage! Amelia's giving the cat cooties!"

There's a roar of laughter behind her and the teacher says, "That's enough, Ryan. Everyone back to their seats. Amelia, cages aren't for kissing—you know that."

She doesn't move.

She's not kissing my cage; she's trying to say something. She's getting up her nerve.

Finally she does. "If you were my cat, I'd name you Benjamin Franklin," she whispers.

And just like—after I've heard my own name out loud for the first time in months—she disappears.

CHAPTER TEN

"DID YOU HEAR THAT, CHESTER? AMELIA knew my name! Nobody told her, but she knew it."

"Didn't she want to name you Benjamin Franklin?"

"Yes, but that's close enough! Who is Benjamin Franklin, by the way?"

"We've been learning about him in school. He's a man who invented kites and electricity and stoves and rocking chairs and wrote the Declaration of Independence."

"Obviously that's not true, Chester. One person didn't do all those things."

"I think he did. The teacher read us a book that was written by Ben Franklin's mouse."

As fond as I am of him these days, Chester does say silly

things sometimes. "Mice don't write books, Chester. Obviously."

He thinks about it. "This one did. His name was Amos. He says he gave Ben Franklin all his best ideas."

Oh please. "How did he do that?"

"They talked. He was a very smart mouse. And very chatty. Franklin was smart to listen to him." Suddenly this story is a little confusing because I know one fact is true. *Mice are chatty.*

I have to admit, this dampens my mood a bit. If Gus can hear Chester and Ben Franklin can hear Amos, why haven't I found a person who understands me?

I ask Chester this, and he considers for a while. "I think it's pretty unusual for people to understand their pets. I can't think of too many examples."

"Where does Benjamin Franklin live? Maybe we could talk to him, or his mouse."

"I got the feeling he's not alive anymore. In the pictures, he's wearing old-fashioned clothes like tights and wigs."

This sounds ridiculous. "*Why?*"

Chester bites at a gnat. "I'm not sure. Ms. Winger never explained that part."

The more I think about it, the gloomier I feel. How will I

ever find a special connection with Amelia if her parents say no and someone else's parents say yes?

That night, before dinner, Sara tells Marc about (what was for her, I guess) the best part of today—Gus reading his speech aloud. "He did beautifully! The kids were all amazed. They gave him a huge round of applause."

Marc is mostly interested in the same thing I am. "Did you get any takers on the cat?"

"Oh, everyone said they wanted him. Ms. Winger sent home a note saying if any family is sincerely interested, they should get in touch with us."

"They don't have to be that sincere," Marc says. "We don't mind if they're superficial. Has anyone called?"

"Not yet. There was one interesting girl who I've noticed before because she always gloms on to Chester. Her name is Amelia and I've wondered if she might be a friend for Gus."

"Isn't she the one who's so good at math?"

"Yes. She's very bright, but she struggles at school with other things. The teacher says she has anxiety issues. She gets overwhelmed. I think one of the reasons she comes over to Chester so much is to get away from all the other kids. She talks to Chester a lot. I'm hoping that's her way of talking to Gus, maybe."

"Does he respond?"

"Not that I've seen, but he doesn't avoid her the way he does with other kids. There's something different about her."

"Does he ever use his computer to talk to her?"

"Not yet, but I get the feeling if it happens with anyone, it would be her."

Marc makes a face, but I can't tell what it means. "She's the smartest girl in the class and Gus still can't add or subtract and you're thinking she's a candidate for a friend?"

Sara shakes her head and frowns. I'm trying to figure out what these facial expressions mean and I might be getting a little bit better. I'm guessing she's mad. "I don't think kids give each other math tests when they're picking out friends, Marc."

"No, but they notice when other kids do schoolwork on a much lower level than theirs."

"I don't think that's always true. Ms. Winger says she's a complicated girl who's wrestling with a lot of issues herself," Sara says.

Marc's eyebrows go up. "It sounds like that means emotional issues. Gus isn't going to be too great with that."

"No, I know. But he understands anxiety. Chester helps

69

him with that. Maybe there are ways they might be able to help each other."

Marc stares at Sara for a long time and doesn't say anything.

"What is he thinking?" I whisper to Chester.

"He thinks that sometimes Sara has overly optimistic ideas. Especially about Gus making friends," Chester says.

"Is that what you think, too?"

"I think Gus doesn't understand most kids. But Sara's right. Amelia is a little different. She doesn't scare him, even though sometimes she scares other kids."

This is worrying. "How?"

"She cries pretty easily. Sometimes for no reason that anyone can see," Chester says. "She used to have friends, or at least a couple of girls she sat with at lunch, but I don't think she does anymore. I think maybe they had a blowup."

A blowup? What does that *mean*? I turn away from Chester and back to Sara.

"Here's the interesting part, though," Sara says. "Amelia zeroed in on the cat from the moment we walked into the room. She was never more than five feet away, even when all the other kids were pressing in to see him and pet him. She waited and waited and when it was finally her turn, she got really close to his cage. The kids said she was trying to kiss the cage, but she wasn't. She was *talking* to him. And for the first time since we walked in the room, the cat was quiet and listened. Something happened. I'm not sure what exactly. But something."

Behind me, Chester says, "Did you hear that? I was right! Amelia likes you!"

"But what about the other stuff? The blowups and the crying? That sounds worrying."

"She's just a little different than other kids. That's not bad. So is Gus. Sometimes belonging to a kid who is different is better for us. They care about their pets more because they don't have as many human friends."

It's maddening that Chester, a dog, might be thinking more logically than I am. I'm letting my emotions get in the way. They're filling up my brain and not letting me think. I like Amelia because she somehow knew my real name and therefore the real me. And then I worry: if the other children don't like Amelia, there must be a reason. Maybe she is a girl who would do unpredictable things like put clothes on a cat. For the rest of the night, I fling back and forth between these two emotions.

I like Amelia.

I'm scared of Amelia.

By morning, I wonder if Chester was right all along. None of this seems to matter because Amelia's parents haven't called. In fact, nothing matters much because no one else's have either.

CHAPTER ELEVEN

FOR TWO DAYS, AMELIA DOESN'T CALL.

Nor does anyone else.

After Gus and Chester come home from school, I spend most of the afternoon sitting near the phone.

"Are you waiting for it to ring?" Chester asks after I've been there for a while.

"No," I snap. "I'm comfortable here is all."

"Amelia wasn't in school today, in case you're wondering if I saw her. She's been absent a lot lately."

"Is she sick?" People get sick a lot more than animals, with illnesses I don't really understand. I think of cold as a temperature, but apparently it can also be a sickness.

"I don't know. I heard one teacher say there were changes at home that she was dealing with."

"What does that mean?"

"I'm not sure."

Maybe this isn't a bad sign. I've had a lot of changes at home, too. Except mine are changes *of* home.

"One week, Marc," Sara says that night at dinner. "That's it, I promise. Give me one week and if we can't find a home for him, we'll take him to the shelter."

"I wish I could give you more time, but I'm spending half my workday zoned out on allergy medication. Yesterday, I apparently had a whole phone call that I don't remember."

"Seven days. We're going to do this. Right, Puff? We're putting up flyers today in the grocery store and around town. I'm calling a few nursing homes. I think he'd make a great therapy pet. He could spend his whole day in an old person's lap. Can't you picture that?"

I walk swiftly past Chester to demonstrate that I am not looking to be some grandmother's lap blanket. Even Chester looks apologetic: "She's just trying to think of every possibility. She doesn't really want to put you in a nursing home."

It's been three days since my school visit and still, no one has called to ask about adopting me. Proud as I am, I have to admit this hurts.

On the fourth night, I get so low, I curl up next to Chester on his bed. "All those kids raised their hands and said they wanted me. I don't understand."

"Parents don't always listen to their kids," Chester says. "Or they listen but they're too busy. They say 'We'll see,' which means they don't want to think about that right now. I think a lot of parents said 'We'll see' when their kids came home with the flyer about you."

"Does that mean no?"

"Not necessarily. In my experience, sometimes it means you have to wait a long time, but if the kid keeps asking, it means 'Okay, fine. I give up.'"

This is interesting information to have. I wonder if Amelia is at home right now pestering her parents. I keep thinking about her face, pressed up against the bars of my cage. I keep thinking about what Chester said—she might be different, but that's not scary. Sometimes different is better for us.

The next night I sleep on Chester's bed again. If he doesn't stretch out too much, there's plenty of room for me without touching him. I don't like touching other things when I sleep unless I know they're not alive and won't move suddenly. But sleeping with Chester is different. I thought his breathing would drive me crazy, but it turns out it doesn't. Even when it's loud, it's kind of comforting, the way dishwashers are nice to lie near and listen to after a long day. Steady and hummy. Naturally, I wait until the family is in bed to take up my spot. I don't want anyone to see me lying here and say something like, "Aw, look how sweet they are." That wouldn't change anyone's mind about letting me stay; it would just be embarrassing.

Tonight, Chester comes back down from Gus's room and curls up on his bed in the smallest ball he can make of himself, leaving me half the bed. It's so nice I can't look him in the eye as I take my spot.

He doesn't say anything and neither do I.

I haven't been to school and I'm not good at math, but both of us know I only have a few nights like this left. Both of us know that's not a lot.

I don't know how long we've been asleep when a ringing telephone startles us awake. Chester lifts his head. I turn my ears away from the sound. A red light blinks in the darkness and we hear a girl's voice: "Hello, Gus, this is Amelia from school. My mom just said I can have your cat. Unless someone else got him. Then I'll be mad that it took so long for my mom to say yes. I really want your cat. That's all. Okay, bye."

Chester sits up and puts his face closer to me, staying careful not to touch. "How about that!" he says. "I knew she would want you."

It's hard for cats to express emotions. Feeling them makes us uncomfortable, like we might be dirty, so we clean ourselves and wait for the feeling to pass. I've never felt cleaner or fluffier than I have since my visit to school, and now, with Chester watching, I tend to my tail because I don't know what else to do.

I'm so happy and relieved that I fear something terrible might happen, only I don't know what. Could a car drive into this kitchen and run us both over? It doesn't seem likely, but watching Rocky get hit and die in the road was the last time I felt this much at once.

Surprises are scary, even good ones.

They change everything.

You think your life looks one way and then everything is different.

"You'll be okay," Chester whispers. "Living with Amelia might feel confusing at first, but remember how much you didn't like being here when you first came? How you thought I was so dopey?"

I lick my tail furiously. This is too much. What if this is our last night together? What if I have a home but I never see Chester again? Chester falls back asleep soon after this, but I can't. There's too much to worry about.

CHAPTER TWELVE

A FUNNY THING HAPPENS THE NEXT MORN-
ing. No one notices the blinking red light and no one
listens to the message. Sara takes Gus and Chester to school
while I wait on my sofa perch all day for them to return.
They still don't play the message. I get so tired of waiting for Sara to notice that I go over to the machine and sit
down next to it.

"Oh, Puff, no!" Sara says. "No cats on the kitchen counter. You know better than that!"

She lifts me up and drops me unceremoniously on the
ground. "People miss the point of what we're trying to
tell them about ninety percent of the time," I complain to
Chester.

"I know. It's hard," Chester agrees. "We saw Amelia today

at school. She came up to Gus and said 'So?' and he didn't know what she was talking about. I tried to tell him, but he wasn't listening."

"What if they *never* listen to the message?"

"They will."

"But what if they *don't*?"

"You shouldn't worry. They will."

Chester's right. They listen to it that evening. Sara puts her hand over her mouth.

"What does that expression mean?" I whisper to Chester.

"I think it's a combination of surprise and happiness."

"You don't think she looks scared? I think she looks scared."

"Remember, you're not as good at reading faces as I am. No. She's happy for you."

Sara calls back right away and apologizes for the delay. "We just listened to Amelia's message and we're delighted. . . . Yes, I noticed that she felt a special connection with this cat. . . . Yes, he's still available."

I feel another storm of emotions listening to this conversation. After she hangs up, I leave the kitchen. Suddenly I have a lot to do. People I need to say goodbye to.

I sit outside Marc's office for a bit without going in. I don't want to make him sneeze again. He's a nice man, and I wish

I could tell him how sorry I am about all this.

Next I go to Gus's room. Chester is there, as usual, lying on the rug in the middle of the room, keeping an eye on him. I watch them for a while. Chester is concentrating so much on Gus, he doesn't even realize that I'm sitting here in the hallway, watching him. I used to assume that all dogs were dopey, which made me feel sorry for them. I felt the sorriest of all for service dogs because it seemed like they'd agreed to give up their life. Now that I've gotten to know Chester, I feel different. I admire the way he's overcome some of his innate deficits, like useless claws and dull teeth, and figured out smart ways to have an impact on the people around him. I don't think dogs are dopey anymore. They just pretend to be, which I still don't understand.

Here is an example of what makes Chester a good service dog: a lot is happening, but he doesn't get distracted. He keeps doing his job, which is being near Gus in case he needs him. It means he hardly ever does what he wants to do unless Gus is asleep or Gus tells him to leave and closes his bedroom door. Sometimes this happens. I think Gus gets tired of being stared at. I would, too.

But even when that happens, Chester doesn't mind. Sometimes he'll find me or an old rawhide chew, but mostly he waits for Gus to come out and need him again.

I didn't understand any of this when I first got here. Now I do. Chester has a job to do. An important job. Some days go better than others, like when he suggested Gus read his speech out loud so all the kids could hear his voice. He didn't want to brag about it afterward, but I know it felt good. It was a great idea and it worked. When Sara told Marc the story, Chester sat up and listened with both ears.

I admit, I felt a little jealous.

There's a special feeling of accomplishment when you kill a chipmunk and lay it on your family's front porch, but even I can see, this is a different feeling of pride. Once I watched Emily's dad sweep up a mouse I'd left for them and say, "Why does this cat have to *do* these things?" I couldn't tell what his facial expression meant, but as I watched him dump the mouse in a trash bag and carry the bag outside, I wondered: *Is he taking it somewhere to save it?* Now that I've lived with Chester and this family, I know what the answer is—probably not.

If you watch people carefully, you learn a lot of things. You put the pieces of their mysterious, puzzling behavior together. You figure out this surprising fact: I don't think humans like getting dead rodents left on their porch at all.

Watching Chester has taught me that if I want to be part

of a family again, I have to learn what they really need and then I have to figure out a way to give it to them. It's a daunting prospect. Humans are confusing.

Suddenly Chester doesn't seem dopey at all.

CHAPTER THIRTEEN

WE'RE ALL PRETTY NERVOUS WAITING FOR Amelia and her mom to pick me up. Chester has already warned me that Sara might cry because she does that a lot, he says.

"What does crying look like?" I ask, which is silly. I've seen people cry. I'm more anxious than I thought I'd be. I'm not sure why.

"Don't you remember from living with Emily? Kids make noise when they cry; grown-ups usually don't. Sometimes you don't even know they're crying except when you go closer, you can see their faces are wet."

Seeing people cry is horrible. "What are you supposed to *do*?"

"Usually I try to lick away tears, which is fine with Sara,

but Gus hates when I lick his face, so I don't with him."

Lick her tears? "I really hate some of the things you tell me. Maybe it would be better to leave without saying goodbye at all."

"Don't worry. I'll take care of any crying. That's more of a dog's job anyway."

"Fine. Please do."

The problem is, they're late. Neither Chester nor I can tell time, but Sara has asked Marc if he thinks it's a bad sign that they're an hour late. Maybe they've changed their minds?

I've spent so much of this hour bathing myself that my tongue is numb.

They finally show up and Amelia looks the same as she did at school, which is a relief. She's even wearing the same shirt that she was wearing at school the day I met her, which is nice. She doesn't rush right over and pick me up, which I also appreciate. Instead, she stands over me and says, "Hello, Benjamin Franklin. Are you ready to come live at my house?"

Of course I don't answer her. I don't even look at her. I wash myself and hope she understands—I'm nervous about many things: the cat carrier, the car ride, Sara crying.

Chester comes over and bumps her hand for a hello rub.

Amelia's mom is named Connie. Sara gives her a hug and

says, "Thank you so much for this, Connie. You're a life-saver. Literally. We've only had this cat for two weeks and already we're so fond of him. We couldn't bear to give him to a shelter."

Connie says, "Well, Amelia really wants this and she's promised to be the one taking care of him, right, Am? You're going to remember to feed him every day and clean his litter box?"

Amelia doesn't say anything. I don't blame her. Just mentioning litter boxes embarrasses everyone, me most of all.

Sara goes to the cardboard box that she's put together. "Here's his food and his bowl. And this is his litter pan. He's very careful about this. You don't have to worry too much about cat mess with him."

Again with the litter pan talk? Amelia looks in the box but still doesn't say anything. I think she's nervous, but it's hard for me to tell because I'm so nervous.

"We probably shouldn't stay too long," Connie says, jiggling her car keys. "Can we call you if we have any questions?"

"Of course. Let me just get Gus so he can say hello to Amelia and goodbye to the cat."

A few minutes later, Gus comes down, holding his mom's hand, which he doesn't usually do. I wonder if this means he didn't really want to come down.

"Okay, Gus," Sara says. "We have to say hello to Amelia. And then we have to say goodbye to the cat."

We wait. For a long time, he doesn't say anything.

"He likes Amelia," Chester whispers to me. "I know he does. He's just confused. He doesn't understand why she's here."

"Does he know I'm going to live with her?"

"I thought he did. Now I'm not sure."

Even though Chester spends all his time with Gus, there's a lot he doesn't know about him, which always surprises me. The silence keeps going, like Gus will never be able to do what Sara is asking and someone should step in and help him. I look at Chester. "Can you tell him what to say?" I whisper.

He stares at Gus. "I'm waiting."

And then, just when I'm ready to leave the room to get away from all this tension, Gus rocks forward and says, very softly, "Hello, Amelia." And then, after a deep breath, "Goodbye, cat."

Everyone laughs and Sara claps her hands. "Good job, Gus!"

I have to admit, I'm surprised. Except for the speech he read at school, I've never heard Gus say more than yes or no or repeat something he's just heard. Maybe that's what he was doing here, but it feels a little different. He's peeking up at Amelia like he cares what she thinks. I look at her but I can't tell what she's thinking.

I can tell Chester is happy. "I *told* you he liked her."

Connie picks up the box of my things and says they should probably get going. Suddenly I feel as scared as I did when I watched Emily and her family drive off on vacation. I look over at Chester and then at Sara and Gus. *This is my family!* I think. *I don't want to lose them!*

"I know this might sound a little crazy," Sara says. "But would it be possible for Gus and Chester and me to stop by some time and visit the cat?"

I don't think this sounds so crazy. I think it sounds great, but Connie says they'll have to wait for a bit. "We've just moved and we're still getting settled. Our place is kind of a mess. We'll call you, though. A visit sounds nice!"

CHAPTER FOURTEEN

I WANT TO STAY CALM, BUT I can't. Being in cars means you never know which way you're going to slide. You can dig your claws in and you move anyway. It's impossible to stop meowing. I don't know how people get in cars every day, like it's nothing at all.

Amelia turns my carrier so she can put her face in front of the cage door the way she did at school. "You're okay, Benjamin Franklin," she whispers. "You're going to live with us now and I'm going to take care of you."

It's nice to hear her voice and see her lips pressing up against the bars again.

"We already bought you some cat food. I hope you like seafood buffet and chicken giblets. I picked them out myself."

I forget what giblets are, but the seafood buffet sounds

nice. She keeps talking, but it's hard for me to listen and concentrate on not losing what's left of my fur.

After we get home, Amelia takes my carrier into her room and I hear Connie say, "I'll leave you two to get settled."

As much as I hate carriers, it's a little hard to leave them when someone opens the door in an unfamiliar place. Suddenly a plastic cage with metal bars on the door seems better than whatever you might find outside. I'm not sure why.

When I finally step out, Amelia starts talking. Very fast, so it's hard to understand her at first. "I love cats. I've always loved cats. Here's all the books I have on cats." She points to a few piles of books on the floor. There are a lot. She opens one and shows it to me as if maybe I can read, which of course I can't, so she closes it again.

I think maybe she's nervous and talking helps her feel calmer.

She tells me she's loved cats ever since she met one at the zoo when she was six years old, a tiger named Rajah, who looked her right in the eye. He could read her mind, or that's what it felt like anyway. Ever since, she's loved Rajah and all other cats, but she's never owned one because her dad always said no, but now they don't live with her dad anymore, which means she and her mom moved into this apartment and her mom said yes, she could get a cat. "So the best part of not seeing my dad so much is now I can have you instead!"

During this speech, Connie carries my box of things into Amelia's room. "Take a deep breath, sweetheart. Benjamin can't understand fast talking like that."

Amelia rolls her eyes.

"Amelia, I mean it. Take a deep breath."

She does. So do I.

"Now blow out. Slowly." Connie puffs her cheeks out and makes her mouth a tiny O. So does Amelia. They both blow out a few times. I can't make my mouth do this.

"Good," Connie says. "Now why don't you show him a few more things in here and then let him explore the rest of the apartment."

Chester never mentioned anything about Amelia having a problem with fast talking. He only said she's a little bit different, but now I'm wondering about this. Gus was different in a quiet, predictable way. Amelia seems different in a worried, talky way. I wonder if being around her all the time will be hard on my nerves.

Amelia's room doesn't look anything like Emily's room, which was filled with stuffed animals and dolls. Amelia's room has books and notebooks and lots of papers scattered around on the floor. There are also pictures of cats everywhere. Some of them are drawings and some are posters with words written on them. I stop in front of one that Amelia reads out loud: "A cat has nine lives. For three, he plays. For three, he strays. And for three, he stays."

I don't understand that.

"Cats don't *really* have nine lives," she explains, taking a deep breath so she isn't talking quite as fast as she was before. "Cats are just great survivors, which is why people say that. You might be the best survivors in the whole animal kingdom. Mostly because cats are great hunters. You can see in the dark. You can hear better than humans. You can smell with both your nose and your mouth. There are more cats on earth than any other animal except for insects and, like, ocean plankton, maybe."

I certainly don't mind hearing all the reasons cats are great. Although I've never wanted to be a bragger, I've always sensed I might be superior to other animals and it turns out I'm right.

After I've walked around for a while, Amelia goes over to the corner and taps the side of a cardboard box. She doesn't say anything, but I think she wants me to look at what's inside.

I go closer. The top has been cut off so it's easy to peek

in. There's a small pillow at one end and a plastic ball with a bell inside at the other.

"I made you your own room in case you want some privacy," she says. "The pillow is your bed, and Mom let me use my allowance to buy you the ball. I hope you like it."

Even Emily never made anything this nice for me. And although I'm not sure what an allowance is, I know Emily never used one to buy me a cat toy. It's so nice that I have to sit down for a moment and clean my paws.

"There's a door," she says. "If you want to go inside."

She opens a flap in the side of the box and on the inside is a drawing. At first I can't tell what it is, so I move closer and then I have to sit down again. It's a drawing of me. With every detail in the right place: my whiskers, my ears, the little white spot on my forehead.

"You don't have to go inside," she says. "I know some cats like boxes, but some don't. It's okay."

I love boxes. I always have. I love them even more than empty grocery bags, which were always my mother's favorite. "Empty boxes are better," my siblings and I would say, and she'd shake her head and walk away.

I think about my brothers and sisters now. I wonder if any of them got lucky enough to end up in a home with someone who made them a box like this. I hope they did.

❀ ❀ ❀

As much as I love it, it turns out playing with a ball inside a box is exhausting. It never stops moving and making a little tinkling sound that sets my heart racing. I can only do it for a few minutes and I have to take a break.

I leave my box and keep looking around the room.

"Sorry about the mess," Amelia says. "My mom said I had to clean up before you came, but I was too excited, so we got in a fight."

Even though I know she can't hear me, I reassure her: *Don't worry about cleaning up for me. I'm extremely tidy about my own appearance, but I like messy spaces. It means I have papers to sleep on and underwear drawers to explore.*

When I walk over some papers, Amelia tells me it's fine to sit there because she doesn't care about them. "That's a problem set I'm doing for the Math Olympiad. Those are on probability, which I don't really understand."

She doesn't like geometry either, which she tells me when I move to a different piece of paper. I don't know what these words mean, but I do like relaxing on a piece of a crinkly paper. I start giving myself a bath to let her know that I'm happy to be here and if she wants to take a break from talking for a while, it would be okay.

For a while, she's quiet, and then, out of nowhere, she

makes a funny sound—a sort of gasp, like she can't breathe.

I look up. I don't understand.

Her eyes are wet.

She's crying, which doesn't make any sense. Her stories have been about happy things like how great cats are until she started talking about math. Is it possible that math is sadder than I think? It's hard to tell what's going on.

Why are you crying? I ask.

She doesn't answer. She finds a Kleenex and blows her nose, which is not a sound that I enjoy hearing. I spent all morning worried that Sara might cry when I left, but I never considered the possibility that Amelia might cry after I got here.

I don't know what to do. Licking her face like Chester suggested seems like a bad idea.

I stand up and circle around the paper I've been sitting on. My tail looks terrific now. I wave it around a bit, hoping this might cheer her up. It doesn't.

I venture closer. Gus doesn't like Chester touching him too much, but touching him a little sometimes helps. I try an experiment. I bump Amelia's leg with my head and step back. I study her face. I can't tell what she's thinking. My tail hasn't helped, nor has my head bump.

I jump up and sit on the bed beside her. Even sitting this

close to her face, it's hard for me to look at it and guess what the problem is.

Connie knocks on the door and Amelia dries her face with her sleeve like she doesn't want her mom to see her crying.

"Is everything okay in there?" Connie says.

No! I say. *She's crying! I don't know* why *or what to* do.

"Yeah, it's great," Amelia says, though her face is still red and her eyes are still wet. "Everything's great."

CHAPTER FIFTEEN

I'M SURPRISED. AFTER AMELIA STOPS CRYING, everything seems okay.

She and Connie eat dinner together at the kitchen table and watch me walk around the living room, which is also full of boxes, some of them on their side, so I have my choice of hideouts, which is fun.

After dinner, Connie asks Amelia if she wants to practice her math. I'm across the room, but I stop walking. *No, Not math!* I say. *Math makes her cry!*

"Okay," Amelia says softly.

Connie gets up. "Let me get my calculator."

When she comes back, Amelia closes her eyes. I can't tell if this means she's dreading this, or falling asleep.

"What's 1,729 plus 326?" Connie asks, punching in the numbers.

"2,055," Amelia says very quickly without opening her eyes.

After a moment, Connie says, "Wow, sweetheart. That's right!" Amelia can do the problem faster than her calculator.

"How about 624 minus 471?"

"153," Amelia says.

Connie is still punching in the numbers. "Right!" she says again, smiling. "How do you *do* this?"

"I don't know," Amelia says.

They go through more problems with longer numbers. Connie claps and laughs every time she gets another one right.

Amelia doesn't look as happy as her mom. After a while, she sighs and looks toward her bedroom door. "Can I be done now?"

"Of course, sweetheart. You did a great job. I can't wait to tell your dad how good you've gotten at this."

Amelia doesn't wait for me to follow her back to our bedroom, so I stay in the living room to look around. They live in something called an apartment, which seems to be smaller than most houses I've seen. They have two bedrooms, one of which, apparently, I'm not allowed to go in. "I'm sorry, Benjamin," Connie says. "But I keep all my work things in there and I can't have your fur mess get mixed in with my computer stuff. So you're not allowed in my bedroom."

What fur mess? I ask, but of course she doesn't answer.

After spending all this time with Chester, I realize that it's lonely having no one understand me.

Unfortunately, Connie's got some *more* rules she wants to tell me about. I'm not allowed on counters. I also can't eat people food. And this: "We can't let you go outside, I'm afraid. Supposedly pets aren't allowed in this apartment complex, so we have to make sure no one ever sees you."

I'm sitting in a window when she tells me this, noticing a tree that seems to have a perfect perch for keeping an eye on both the birds overhead and the rodents below. There's also a small garden with some bark mulch that I wouldn't mind rearranging.

"I told Amelia, a big grown cat might not like staying inside all the time, but she said no, you wouldn't mind."

Oh dear. This news is more upsetting than any rules about not jumping on a counter or eating people food. I remember a story my mother used to tell us about a neighbor cat who never went outside. Occasionally, he sat in a window and mocked passing cats with names like Ruffian! Scamp! No one had any idea what he was saying, so the other cats ignored him. Even calling him a name didn't seem worth the effort when he was so far away and so unthreatening. Then one day a house sitter urged him to come outside, using bits of food lined up in a trail into the grass. He was so disoriented, he fell off the front porch, and when he got to the grass, he couldn't find any of the food she'd laid out. "Oh, we all had to laugh at that spectacle," my mother told us. "Apparently if it wasn't shaped like a can and offered in a bowl, he didn't think he should eat it!"

The story was meant as a warning: Never let this happen to you. Keep up your hunting skills. Tend to your claws so they're sharp enough for tree-climbing. You're a cat, first and foremost, not a piece of furniture or a home decoration.

Remembering all this makes my tail twitch nervously. When I lived with Emily, I didn't spend a lot of time outside—I was still a kitten, capable of making a mountain out of sofa cushions—but I certainly went out once a day, unless it was raining (no cat likes to be caught in the rain). At Chester's house, I didn't go outside much, but that was only because I didn't want to ruin the groomer's efforts. I had the *option*. I went out *occasionally*, along with Chester, who had no other way to go to the bathroom.

I make my way back to Amelia's bedroom, where she's on her bed, writing in a notebook.

I think there's been a mistake, I say. *Your mother says I'm not allowed outside, but cats need to spend at least a little time outdoors. The reason we're such good survivors is that we keep up our skills: hunting, foraging, that kind of thing. Plus, we have to establish our territory. We do that by spraying, which might sound silly to you, but is very, very important to us. If we don't establish boundaries, every other cat will just walk willy-nilly over our lawns and into our window views. This kind of thing is very upsetting to a cat. Very.*

Suddenly I wonder if I sound like Amelia: talking too fast, or going on too long. It's hard not to with such an important topic.

Amelia doesn't look up from whatever she's working on.

Chester said it took a lot of practice before Gus understood him. He said it might not seem like Amelia hears anything at first, but I should keep trying. "If she's meant to be your person, eventually she'll understand what you're saying."

Clearly this isn't happening yet. In fact, I'm not sure she's noticed that I've come back in the room.

I try again. *Excuse me, Amelia, but I'd like to negotiate some of the rules I'm hearing about. I'm worried because indoor cats get laughed at by other cats. We can really be quite mean to each other.*

I remember the other children at school making fun of Amelia when she whispered into my cage. Surely, if she can hear me at all, she'll sympathize with this.

I wait for a long time. She never looks up.

CHAPTER SIXTEEN

I'VE GOT TO DO SOMETHING. I spend the next three days looking for escape routes, but I don't think there are any. Every open window has a screen in it and every time I press hard on one, my claws get caught.

Amelia is scared of my claws so each time I get stuck, she yells, "MOM! BENJAMIN'S ATTACHED TO THE SCREEN AGAIN!"

The third time this happens, I abandon my idea of a window escape.

There's the front door, of course, but it isn't opened very often or for very long. Mostly people use it to leave and come back. There's not much of a way to anticipate when either of these things are going to happen.

In between hatching plans to escape, I'll admit that

Amelia and I have been having some fun together. She'll crumple up her math homework and throw it on the floor, where I'll bat it around until it rolls under her bed, which means we can both forget about it. What she likes much more than math, I've learned, is drawing, which she's very good at. Watching her draw is fun because I can bat at the pencil a bit and then try to guess what the picture is before she finishes. *A hand!* I'll say. Or *A cat!* These are usually good guesses because she likes drawing hands and cats. Sometimes she'll draw trees and nature, but she never draws people because people have faces, which are hard to draw.

"Eyes and mouths are really hard," she tells me.

You're good at drawing cat faces, I point out.

"Cats are easier because cat's noses are triangles and cats have fur to cover mistakes." *Wait a minute*, I think. *Did she just hear me?*

I move a little closer. *If you just heard me, I'd love to talk about a few things. Like going outside occasionally. I don't have to do it a lot. Just every now and then.*

I wait. Nothing.

Maybe we could go out together? You could draw a tree while I climb it!

I wait some more. Still nothing.

I know she wants to make me happy. I can tell by the way

she makes me dinner every night with dry food and wet food in separate dishes so the food doesn't touch. "I don't like my food to touch," she tells me. "Crunchy and soft at the same time is confusing in my mouth."

I hadn't thought of it quite this way before, but she's absolutely right. Soft and crunchy at once is confusing. She also likes to give me a variety of flavors and apologizes any time liver is on the menu. "It smells terrible, but Mom says we can't waste these cans, so you're getting some liver tonight."

I didn't mind liver until she pointed out the smell and the slimy texture. Now I agree.

Amelia takes good care of me, which means that even though I keep making my case to her—that going outside is good for cats, that three rooms isn't a lot of space for a cat to spend his day in—I don't blame her for not understanding.

It's hard for Amelia to understand my problems when she has quite a few of her own to worry about. Most days when she gets home from school, I hear about the kids who say mean things and won't let her eat lunch with them in the cafeteria. The worst are two girls she used to be friends with—Maura and Shayna—who like to point out when her socks don't match or her hair has a knot in the back. They say they're only trying to help, but sometimes they don't say these things *to* her, they say them *near* her, which makes it seem like they're not trying to help at all, they're just making fun of her. It's hard for her to tell.

Amelia admits that she *has* made some pretty big mistakes in the past. While she draws, she tells me stories. When her hands are busy, it's not fast-talking stories that are hard to follow. She tells me that she used to go over to Maura's and Shayna's houses sometimes, which was fun at first, but then less fun because they never wanted to do the same things. The other girls liked acting out books Amelia had never read and didn't care about. She doesn't like stories with magic and witches and make-believe things. She likes cats and facts and nonfiction books. "They used to say I was only allowed to talk about cats for ten minutes and then I had to stop. Can you believe that?"

I don't know how long ten minutes is, but I do know that Amelia likes to talk a lot. For me, it's fine. I also don't mind hearing more about cats. It's a subject I'm interested in.

On one of those playdates, Amelia accidentally said something rude when Maura's mom offered her graham crackers and cream cheese. Amelia said, "No, that would make me throw up," because it was true. Some foods are gluey and get stuck in her throat.

Maura told her it was rude to say things like that when people offer you food. So at Shayna's house, Amelia told her dad all the foods she couldn't eat right after she arrived. He listened to the list and at the end said, "Wow. I might have to run to the grocery store," and laughed.

Again, Maura said she was being rude. "You don't even know if he was going to offer you something."

They stopped inviting her over in the fall, which probably just as well because going over to other people's houses had started to make her nervous. Sometimes she had to say, "Can I call my mom? I think it's time for me to go home."

She wasn't sure why, exactly, but sometimes she felt like she had to go home, even if she'd only been at the friend's house for half an hour.

One terrible time, she cried and said she was scared someone might die if she didn't get home. That was stupid, she realized afterward, especially when Maura's mom bent down and said, "Is someone sick?"

No one was sick, but Amelia had been feeling like this since her parents told her they were separating last fall. Like she couldn't control anything and people you liked or even loved could disappear at any time.

She says she's fine not going over to other people's houses anymore, but being at school without any friends is hard. She has no one to talk to at recess and no one to eat lunch with either. She asked Maura and Shayna if they could just be friends at school and they said okay, but for the next week of lunches, all they did was make suggestions for her to work on. Her hair, her clothes, even her laugh. "You snort a little when you laugh," Shayna told her. "Some people have been saying you should work on it, is all."

For a while, Amelia tried following their advice. She stopped wearing her purple shirt three days in a row. She tried not to laugh too loud or too often. She even stopped herself from talking about cats. ("It's weird when you do that," Maura said. "All those details about jaguars and pumas. Other people don't really care.") To keep track of all these suggestions, she wrote them down in her journal, which she read to me one afternoon: "1) Talk about fun things, not cats. 2) Don't sigh really loud when other people ask questions that seem dumb. 3) Be positive, not negative. 4) Look around at the way other kids dress. Try wearing the same things."

In the end it was too hard. Changing yourself to win back old friends doesn't work and it also doesn't help you make any new friends.

I think about something Chester once said: "Yes, the other kids are sometimes mean to Amelia, but she can be mean, too. Once she told Soon-Yi her lunch smelled bad and she shouldn't let her mom pack kimchi again because the smell might make other people throw up."

Even I can see how this was a mistake. Once I asked Rocky how he could eat a marshmallow with pine needles and road tar stuck to it. "Never comment on others' food," he said, licking his fingers and smacking his lips. "Everyone's mouth tastes things differently. To me, this is delicious."

"Making friends is too hard," Amelia tells me after I've been there for a week. "And it never works. Either they make me mad or I make them mad. That's the only thing that happens."

I understand this because cats are more comfortable having a quick fight and walking away than we are making friends or talking to each other. At least I've always felt this way, until I remember Genghis Khan and the ways he helped me even though we'd always been sworn enemies. I also think about Rocky and how I probably wouldn't have survived without him. And Chester, who saved me by finding Amelia.

Friends can be helpful sometimes, I say.

When she doesn't hear me, I touch her arm with my paw.

"Oh, I know you're my friend, Benj. That's enough for me. I don't want any others."

CHAPTER SEVENTEEN

SOME OF AMELIA'S STORIES ARE ABOUT her dad.

He's the one who first took her to the zoo and introduced her to cats and Rajah, the tiger. She loved it so much he got a season pass and took her to visit Rajah almost every weekend. "He was probably my best friend until about two months ago when he started going out with this woman Sandy. She came with us to the zoo once and said she didn't like seeing animals in cages. I got mad because Rajah's not in a cage, he's in a domain. She said, 'But he's trapped, it's not a natural setting. Doesn't that seem sad to you?' I said, 'No, because it's not true. They're very careful about the animals they introduce. If he shows any sign of aggression, they remove the other animal immediately, which means it's not a cage, it's a home he's in control of with a family that only includes animals he likes.'"

Afterward, Amelia told her dad she didn't like Sandy. He said, "That's too bad, sweetheart, because I do."

Connie doesn't think Sandy is so bad. "Your dad's not an easy person to be with," she said. "Sandy makes him happy and he's a lot easier to deal with when he's happy."

Amelia isn't sure exactly what her mom means by this. He's a math professor at a school where he doesn't have a lot of friends because the other people in his department waste too much time at faculty meetings arguing about things that aren't important.

He tells her not to worry about other kids saying mean things or refusing to be her friend. "I went to school with those same kids. They made me miserable, but it turns out they don't matter. You think they do, and then you grow up and realize they all work at convenience stores. You wonder why you once cared so much."

I'm not sure what's bad about working at a convenience store.

Her dad is the reason she joined the Math Olympiad team. He told her being a mathlete was the first time he made real friends who he had something in common with. Connie thought it was a great idea, too, but it turns out mathletes are mean in their own way. Amelia is very good—better than anyone else—at mental math, which means adding and subtracting numbers in her head, but she's not good at almost everything else: fractions, geometry, ratios, word problems.

The boys on her team all loved her at first because they thought she'd help them shave time off their group calculations, until a few weeks into practice when they realized this was her only trick, and the only real math skill she had. Once she started getting answers wrong, they told her that she needed to study more and learn what she didn't know. Now, when they see her on the playground, they don't even say hi. They ask if she's done the packet on fractions yet. "That should help with any ratio questions, too. We've noticed both of those are problem areas for you," they say.

When her dad suggested joining the team, he said he'd come over in the evenings and study with her, but never has. He calls and says he's sorry, but he's spending his evenings looking at apartments to move into with Sandy.

So Amelia is stuck on a math team with boys who hate her.

I've been here for two weeks and things at school definitely aren't getting better for Amelia. Today she came home and told me she ate lunch in the cafeteria at the end of the table with the girls she used to be friends with. There were no other seats around and she hoped if she was quiet and told them no cat facts they wouldn't bother her. But they did.

They wanted to talk about me. "They thought it was weird that I adopted Gus's cat and they wanted to know what you were like. They asked if you were as nasty as you seemed at school. I said you were a great cat and very special because you might be a Maine coon, which is one of the best cat breeds of all. They started laughing and said it sounded like you were part raccoon."

This is wrong on so many levels, it's hard to know where to begin. First of all, I was never "nasty." Secondly, what's wrong with raccoons?

I remember these girls and the way they raised their hands and said they all wanted me until I got scared and then they all backed away and said, "Yeah, no thanks."

You need to forget about those girls, I say. *I mean it. They're not worth your time.*

Over dinner, when Connie asks how math practice went, Amelia says. "I don't really like those kids. Everyone sits around trying to sound smart. Some of them never stop talking. Most of what they say, I don't even understand. It's all inside jokes."

I can relate to this problem. When I spent that week sleeping with bats, it seemed as if they never stopped chattering and I never understood half of what they said.

I hate that, I say.

"I just hate that," she says.

Once again, I have to wonder: Did she just hear me? Is that why she repeated it?

Connie is right here, so I can't ask directly. Instead, I try a trick: *If you can hear me, blink twice,* I say.

She doesn't blink.

It's probably a dumb test. She's thinking about the math team now, not me. Still, it's got me thinking.

Later that night, when we're alone in her room after dinner, I ask, *Do your teammates have high, squeaky voices that make them hard to listen to? Because bats do. I once had to spend some time with bats and I hated it.*

I look over at her as I say this. If she answers me, then I'll know: she is my person and I am meant to be helping her.

The problem is she's drawing again, which is what she likes doing the most, or more than math certainly.

She doesn't answer and she doesn't look over at me. Drawing takes all her concentration, or maybe I said too much at once. Chester once said, "People who can hear us don't realize it sometimes. Because we don't technically make a sound, they think it might be their own strange, unexpected thoughts."

Then he said something I still don't understand: "When I talk to Gus, I try to help him think a little differently. More positively, I suppose. Sometimes I just sit beside him and think of hopeful things."

It can't hurt to give this a try, so I do: *I hope that you don't have to stay with this math team if you don't want to and I hope that someday I can go outside again.*

I don't think Chester included his own hopes in there, but maybe that's the difference between dogs and cats. Maybe I can try to help Amelia and, while I'm at it, help myself, too.

CHAPTER EIGHTEEN

THE NEXT NIGHT AT DINNER, WHEN Connie asks about her day, Amelia says softly, "Not very good."

"Why? What happened?"

"I don't want to talk about it," Amelia says, pushing her plate away. Recently I've noticed Amelia hasn't been eating very much. Even when Connie is careful about not letting any food touch on her plate, Amelia doesn't eat much from her separate piles.

She also doesn't say anything for the rest of the meal. After dinner, Connie suggests watching Amelia's favorite DVD. "We could show Benjamin. I bet he'll love it."

It turns out her favorite DVD is a documentary about cats, which I do love! In the past, I had trouble watching shows about animals because I'd tap and tap at the animal on-screen and could never get its attention. Then Chester explained they couldn't hear me, so now I sit back and watch without worrying about getting anyone's attention.

I learn even more than I do when Amelia reads cat facts from her books before we fall asleep. The most surprising new fact I learn is that all cats are part of the feline family, which also includes lions, tigers, cheetahs, and panthers! I knew tigers looked like me, but I never knew about the others. Emily and I used to watch *The Lion King* all the time and she never said a thing.

We're all cousins, apparently, which gives us some important things in common. As Amelia pointed out on my first day: sharp claws and teeth, which make us good tree climbers, plus great hearing and eyesight, which make us good hunters. It's exciting to watch my cheetah cousin chase down antelope in Africa and catch one. Even though a cheetah looks smaller and the antelope have horns and hooves, they're no match for a feline!

I feel a little sorry for Chester when the video talks about dogs' cousins, which are mostly wolves. I remember the old stories Emily's mother read, where no one liked wolves. In fact, they were always the biggest problem in the story, blowing down houses and eating people's chickens.

If I ever see Chester again, I'll try not to mention this.

Over the next few days, it's hard for me to tell how Amelia's time at school is going because she doesn't say a lot. Her dinners with Connie have gotten so quiet that I've started sitting in an empty chair at the table to help with conversation. "Look, Amelia, I think Benj wants a plate of his own," Connie said the first time I did this. They both laughed, though I didn't see what was so funny. I *would* like a plate of my own.

Usually when I join them for dinner, they talk a little more, so maybe that's good.

Today is Saturday, which should be good because it means Amelia doesn't have school and there's no chance for other kids to say mean things to her, but she seems quiet again. She spends the morning sitting in her room, but she hasn't even opened the sketchbook that she usually works on. Instead of reading or drawing, she kicks the side of her bed with her shoes. Maybe there's something wrong with her shoes or with the bed, I'm not sure.

Connie opens the door and leans in. "I don't know what's going on with your dad or why we haven't heard from him yet. I'm calling him now. We'll figure this out."

I follow Connie out to the kitchen so I can hear what she says. "Amelia is waiting and we haven't heard from you,

Jack. Please call and let us know what's going on."

I go back to Amelia's room and ask, *Was he going to take you to the zoo?* She kicks the bed so hard I worry that maybe she's hurt her foot.

I move a little closer and experimentally bat at one of her shoelaces. She stops swinging her foot and lies back on the bed. I jump up beside her and try one paw, then another, on her chest. I used to lie on chests a lot because heartbeats are nice and generally you'll get an ear rub when you're close to someone's face. I haven't with Amelia because she's usually too busy—reading or drawing or moving around. Plus, I'm not sure she'd like it. I've sat in her lap when we watch TV, and even though she likes it at first, eventually she always pushes me off.

This time she doesn't push me away, so I slip my whole self onto her chest and curl up quickly. I close my eyes so maybe she'll think I'm asleep and let me stay even longer.

Her dad was supposed to see her today and he forgot. I haven't met him yet but she must care about him because she's doing the math team, even though she doesn't like math. I wish I had some good advice like Chester probably would. Unfortunately, I have no experience with these things. I never knew who my father was. I'm not sure what math even is. *It sounds hard* is all I can say.

I still don't think she can hear me, but she's scratching behind my ears, which I do enjoy. I start purring and for a long time, we lie like this: me on her chest, her on her back.

Finally I say, *Chin rubs are nice, too,* and lift my chin up as a clue. She scratches there and my purr motor starts up again. I don't think I've helped with her problems much, but for me, this is lovely.

CHAPTER NINETEEN

"I FINALLY TALKED TO YOUR DAD last night," Connie says the next morning. "He's very sorry about yesterday. He had a fight with Sandy, so you can probably guess—he got distracted, and by the time he remembered what day it was, he was in a bleak mood and didn't think you'd want to see him. He promises he'll make it up to you. He really does feel terrible, honey. Maybe I can ask him to stop by and help with your math this week?'

Amelia sighs and rolls over in bed. For the first time since I got here, I slept on her bed last night, not in my cardboard box bedroom. I made sure I didn't crowd Amelia. I never like getting touched in my sleep and I suspect she doesn't either.

Now I step closer. *Maybe now's the time to tell her that you don't like math*, I suggest.

She doesn't say anything.

"I have a surprise that I hope you'll like," Connie says. "I called Sara and asked if she and Gus and Chester could stop by on Tuesday afternoon. She said yes, which means we have to clean up before they come. All these papers and books need to be put away. But you'd like to see them, right?"

Amelia doesn't say anything, so I fill in. *That's great news! Chester's coming!* I can tell him my problems and maybe some of Amelia's problems, too. Maybe he'll have some ideas on how Amelia can get along better with other kids.

Even as I think this, though, I look around the room. There are *a lot* of papers and books. I think it might take a long, long time to clean up this room.

On Monday, Amelia comes home from school in a fast-talking, wound-up, pacing mood. I haven't seen her quite this riled up before. "The mathletes don't want me on their team anymore. They say I get too mad and I overreact, but the only time I get mad is when Trevor says, 'Time's up, Amelia! Time's up!' even though we're practicing without a timer, so how does he know my time's up?"

"Take a breath, baby."

"I don't want to take a breath! I want to quit the math team!"

Connie's eyes go wide. Amelia's never said this out loud before, even though I've been thinking it a lot so that maybe she would.

For her mom, this is a surprise. "You can't quit, sweetheart. The Olympiad is in two weeks. They need you. You're an important part of the team."

"No, I'm not! I can't do anything except mental math! I don't understand ratios or geometry or any of those other things."

I've heard this before, but apparently Connie hasn't. "Ms. Winger says you're so good at math. You're the best fifth grader in the school."

"Compared to other fifth graders, maybe, but not compared to other mathletes! They try to teach me those other topics, but I don't really care so I don't learn them. I'm NOT good, I'm bad and they hate me! All of them!"

For a long time, Connie doesn't say anything. She keeps her hand over her mouth and shakes her head like there's something she wants to say but isn't sure she should. Finally she takes her hand down. "Okay, sweetheart. You keep saying that nobody at school likes you anymore and everyone is mean to you, but I've talked to your teachers and they say it's not *true*. They say kids treat you the same way they've always treated you. I think you might be imagining some things and making them worse than they are."

Well, this is a surprise. I don't know much about school, but I was there for one day and I saw kids making fun of Amelia when she got too close to my cage and talked to me. I also saw them be mean when she walked away. I wish there was a way to tell Connie that Amelia isn't imagining her problems, but she also isn't helping them.

Later that night, Amelia comes to the table for dinner, but she doesn't eat much and neither one of them laughs when I take my seat in the chair next to her.

After dinner, Connie asks if Amelia wants to watch the cat documentary again.

I'm beginning to feel bad for Connie, who is only trying to help, but Amelia doesn't see it this way because instead of answering, she goes to her room and shuts the door.

The next morning Amelia is quiet until it's almost time for her to leave, and then she walks into the kitchen, where Connie is drinking a cup of coffee, and says, "I don't think I should go to school today."

Connie shakes her head. "No, sweetheart, we're not going to start this again. Remember, we made a deal? I let you stay home for a while during the move because all these transitions were so hard for you, but we made a promise that we weren't going to do this every time something hard happens at school. I've thought about this and I think you should go in today, and when it's time for math team practice, you should tell them you're very good at some things, like doing long addition problems in your head, but there are other things you haven't learned yet and you can't do. Everyone will understand, because you're being honest. They'll probably be relieved and they'll talk about the math areas they're not good at either."

Amelia shakes her head.

It's not a bad idea, I say to her. *You should think about it.*

Amelia shakes her head again. "No, Mom. I can't. Something bad is going to happen if I go to school today."

"That's not true, Amelia. That's your imagination making up scary stories. You mustn't let your fears get too big. Remember all the things we've talked about? If someone says something mean to you, walk away and tell a teacher. If it happens on a playground, you tell a recess monitor, right?"

I see Amelia's hands curling up into fists again, but I don't think Connie sees this.

"No one's going to hurt you, okay?"

Connie's missing something important. Amelia isn't worried about what other kids might do to her today. Amelia is scared about what *she* might do.

❀ ❀ ❀

For the rest of the morning, Connie and I pace nervously. Usually she works in her bedroom, but today she moves her laptop to the kitchen table. Usually I sit in Amelia's window, but today I sit in the living room window.

Connie gets up and walks to the kitchen a lot; I move to the back of the sofa and turn around a lot.

It doesn't help to watch Connie be anxious, so I go back and curl up in the cardboard bedroom Amelia made for me. Usually cats love playing in boxes but don't love sleeping in them. We'd rather be higher up, with a view of our environment. In the beginning, I only slept in here at night so Amelia would know I appreciated the effort she'd made. Now I find myself spending time here during the day because it reminds me of how nice Amelia can be. I wish the other kids at school could see this side of her. I don't know if she would consider making a cardboard box for each of them with drawings on the wall of their faces. If she did, I bet they would start to see her differently.

CHAPTER TWENTY

I'M JARRED AWAKE BY THE PHONE, which hardly ever rings during the day. I hear Connie in the kitchen, and right away I know something bad has happened. "Oh no, I'm so sorry. . . . Yes, okay. I'll come get her right now. . . . Yes, I'll make a doctor's appointment."

A doctor? Is she sick?

After Connie hangs up, she makes another call and says she needs to make an appointment for her daughter. "Yes, it's an emergency. There's been an incident at school where she lashed out at another student. Apparently she had a pencil in her hand and she drew blood. I'm sure it wasn't intentional but even so, she's being asked to stay home for the next three days."

Oh, this is terrible. It's exactly what she was afraid of this morning.

"I don't know what triggered the episode. She's been having a harder time at school lately, which has made her more antagonistic with other kids, but I don't know why."

I do. I think about the way cat fights flare up out of nowhere. Our first instinct is to fight, even with cats we hardly know. Only afterward does it occur to us how foolish it all is when we could be friends, helping each other instead. I think it comes from being scared all the time, even though we don't want to admit it.

But we are. We're scared all the time.

So is Amelia.

Connie doesn't come back with Amelia for a long time. When they finally walk in the door, I almost don't recognize Amelia. Her eyes look glazed over and her legs move slowly, like she's walking through mud. She leans on her mom like if she didn't, she might fall over.

In her room, Connie helps Amelia take off her shoes and lie down. I've never seen Amelia like this—hardly moving, not talking. Her eyes are open but everything else is asleep.

It scares me. I know Connie is scared, too, even though she says calming things. "You can stay in here with Benjamin as long as you'd like. You don't have to worry about school tomorrow or the next day either."

I spend the next hour on the bed watching Amelia carefully. She falls asleep for a while, or else she just closes her eyes. *It's over now,* I tell her. *That's the important thing. You're home and you're safe and it's over.*

Except it's not over.

I overhear Connie on the phone with Amelia's dad, explaining what happened and telling him about the visit with the doctor. "Yes, I told him none of the anxiety medications we've tried have worked, they only make her more agitated. I told him about the move and the changes in our situation. He thinks the problem might be more than that, Jack. He can't diagnose her but he wants us to take her to a neurologist and ask if this might be autism."

Autism? I think. That can't be right. That's what Gus has.

"He says a lot of professionals are starting to think that autism has been underdiagnosed in girls because it looks different with them than it does with boys. Girls are also better at covering up their challenges. He showed me a list of symptoms and I have to say, Amelia checks a lot of boxes. The more this doctor talked about it, the more sense it made. He described something called masking, which girls on the spectrum do a lot. They copy other girls and pretend to like the same things so they can have a few friends. They can get pretty good at it, but it's exhausting and eventually the effort wears them down and they fall apart." She takes a deep breath. I think she's trying not to cry. "That's what's happened, Jack. She's fallen apart. If you saw her—I can't even describe it. She's almost catatonic."

I'm sitting at her feet, listening to all this, trying to put the pieces together. I've never heard the word *catatonic* before, but I assume it means "catlike," which doesn't sound so bad to me. But autism is more confusing. In lots of ways Amelia doesn't seem like Gus at all. He hardly talks and she talks so much that her mom has to remind her to take a breath and slow down. But they do have similarities. He likes staring out the window and doesn't act like other boys. Amelia likes cats and doesn't act like other girls.

Connie is still talking. "I tried to talk to Amelia about it on the way home from the doctor, but she really shut down. I don't think she wants another label or another reason why she's different. She asked if she could take a pill and be more like other kids. I told her we would never want her to be anything besides herself and she said, 'I'd rather be anything else.' Oh, Jack, it's breaking my heart. . . ."

It's too hard to listen anymore or watch Connie cry.

I go back to Amelia's room, where she's fallen asleep, even

though it's the afternoon and still light outside. I jump up on the bed to make sure she's still breathing and also make sure she hasn't changed into somebody else. She still looks the same and smells the same, thank heavens.

I don't want Amelia to wish she was someone different. Just the idea scares me.

I go back to the living room, where Connie is still talking to Amelia's dad. "I just wish she could find one real friend. Someone she could be herself with who wouldn't mind if she talked about cats for hours on end or said the wrong thing now and again. Obviously that's not those old friends. . . . That's what set her off today. Apparently they made fun of her shoes. Obviously, they didn't deserve to be attacked, but why can't they just leave her *alone*?"

The shoe detail surprises me. Amelia doesn't care enough about her clothes to be upset when other kids make fun of them.

Just then the doorbell rings.

She hangs up and opens the front door. It's Chester and Gus! We forgot that it's Tuesday! I stand behind Connie as she opens the door. "Oh, Sara, I'm so sorry! Amelia came home from school sick today. She's in her room asleep right now. I should have called you sooner and I completely forgot—"

By the look of it, Chester knows what's really going on.

He leans his head in to find me. "Is Amelia okay?"

"No," I say. "Did you see what happened?"

"Not really. She scratched Shayna, though Maura was the one who'd said something mean."

"Was it about her shoes?"

"I don't think so. I don't think Amelia cares that much if people make fun of her clothes. She cares about other things."

That's what I was thinking! It's nice to have Chester confirm this.

Above us, the mothers are still talking. "We'll try again another time," Sara says. "Tell Amelia we hope she feels better soon." Sara takes Gus's hand and starts to move back from the door, only Gus doesn't want to leave. He plants his feet and moans when his mom tries to pull him away.

Sara says, "Gus, we can't see Amelia today. She's sick. We'll come back another time when she's feeling better."

Sara takes a step and pulls at Gus's hand. He digs in harder.

Chester looks at me. "He wants to see Amelia. He's worried about her."

"She's asleep right now," I tell Chester. "She wasn't talking when she got home and she looked terrible. I don't think it's a good time for him to see her."

Gus keeps rocking in the doorway. He refuses to move even though his mom is pulling him away. I think of another idea. "Maybe he could come in and use the bathroom. Would it help if he saw her apartment?"

"It might."

Gus has a sign for when he needs to use the bathroom. I know it pretty well because he used it during dinners when he got tired of his parents asking him questions. Chester repeats my suggestion and he uses it now.

Sara says, "I'm so sorry about this, Connie, but would it be okay if Gus came in and used your bathroom before we go? We won't stay long, I promise."

"Of course," Connie says, and looks behind her. I know she's embarrassed about the unpacked boxes and the general mess.

Sara steps in and bends down to say hello to me. "How are you doing, Puff?"

I'm happy to see her—no matter what she calls me—but I can't waste what little time we have. I need to get Chester's advice. I step over to where he's sitting, outside the bathroom. Even though there's a door between them, he wants to keep his eye on Gus. He can't help himself. This is how he operates.

"Amelia's mom took her to a doctor who thinks she might be autistic. Sometimes it looks different in girls, I guess. What do you think?"

"I'm not a neurologist, Franklin. She should take her to one."

Chester never stops surprising me. How does he know what kind of doctor she needs? Then I remember: he goes to all of Gus's doctors' appointments with him.

"She will, but it takes a long time to get an appointment. I'm trying to figure out what we should do in the meantime." I think about what Connie said to Amelia's dad. Maybe Chester can help with this idea. "Amelia needs to find a friend," I tell him. "Just one real friend who she can eat lunch with and spend recess with who won't overreact when she says the wrong things or talks too much about cats, because that's going to happen. That's who Amelia is."

Chester turns away from the bathroom door and looks at me. "Gus is her friend," he says, like the answer is obvious.

"Of course he is, but I'm talking about another girl who shares some of her interests. Like a *real* friend she can get together and do things with—" I stop myself.

I look at Chester's face. For the first time I think maybe I can recognize an expression: I've hurt his feelings. Even though Sara suggested this weeks ago, I've never considered

Gus as a prospective friend for Amelia for obvious reasons: He doesn't really talk. Or respond to other kids. More importantly, he doesn't seem interested in *having* a friend.

I don't say any of this to Chester, of course. Maybe I don't have to—we both know all those points.

Except there's also this: Gus is here now. Making excuses to stay. Maybe he remembers the bad day she had and now he's worried.

Maybe, in his own way, he's the truest friend she has.

"You're right," I whisper. "Gus is a good idea. I'm sorry I didn't think of it before."

Inside the bathroom, the toilet flushes.

If I remember right, Gus can spend a lot of time in the bathroom with water running. I never judged him for this. If I could turn on a faucet, I'd spend a lot of time in bathrooms, too.

Eventually, the bathroom door opens.

Amelia's door opens, too. Maybe she was woken up by the voices. Suddenly, she's standing in the hallway. She looks confused.

Even Chester, who doesn't like to say mean things, has to admit: "She looks terrible, Franklin."

I don't need to hear this: I can see it for myself. Her eyes are red and her mouth hangs open, but that's not even the worst part. The worst part is that she doesn't seem to register that Chester and Gus are here. She's moving toward the bathroom, but Gus is in her way.

"Amelia, wait!" Connie calls. "Gus is coming out now. Can you say hello?"

She can't. A sound comes out of Amelia's throat, but it's not any words. It's a high-pitched whine.

Gus's hands fly up to his ears.

Chester turns his head to get away from it.

"Amelia, stop!" Connie says. "Go back to your room— they aren't staying."

Sara reaches for Gus but keeps her voice calm. "It's okay, Gus. We're not going to stay. We'll come back and visit when Amelia's feeling better."

Amelia won't stop making her sound. The longer it goes on, the worse it gets. Gus wants to get away, I can tell, but he's scared to come out of the bathroom.

Chester stands near Gus. *It's okay*, he says to him. *She's just upset. Like you get upset sometimes. She'll be okay.*

I think Sara's worried that if she pulls Gus out of the bathroom, he'll start screaming, too, so she walks to the front door and opens it. "Walk over to me, Gus!" she calls to him. "Amelia's all right. She's just had a hard day is all. We'll come back when she's feeling better."

It's nice of Sara to sound reassuring like this, but Gus is still frozen by Amelia's terrible racket. We all are. I wish I had hands to cover my ears like Gus is doing.

Just as I think this, Gus starts making his own version of the noise.

I can't stand it.

I run toward Sara and realize she's standing in front of the door that opens up to the outside. There're a few shrubs, some potted plants, and beyond those, a parking lot. I don't even think about what I'm doing. I move quickly and suddenly I'm outside, hiding in a bush.

I've been waiting for this chance forever and now I have it.

For a few seconds, it's thrilling to feel dirt under my paws and branches on my back. Then I run out of dirt. There's a row of parked cars ahead of me. What am I doing? I've made my escape because I couldn't stand the noise, but now I'm here without a clear plan.

From my leafy hiding spot, I see Sara's legs first. And then Chester beside her. He lifts his nose in the air. Can he smell me? Is he going to give me away? He walks over to my bush where I'm hiding and—I can't believe it—lifts his leg. "Chester! What are you *doing*? I'm right here!"

It's too late. He's peed about a foot away from me and left such a puddle it's running in rivulets near my paws. I'll be hours getting this smell out of my fur and my nose.

"Oh, Franklin, I didn't see you! I'm sorry!" He lowers his leg and looks down sheepishly. "What are you doing out here?"

"I'm *escaping* for a few minutes."

"Why?"

"Because I couldn't stand all the noise inside."

"It's quiet now."

I look around. The truth is, I'm scared to go back inside. I'm scared of seeing Amelia so upset that she doesn't act like herself, but I don't want to tell Chester this. "They won't let me go outside, Chester, so I need to escape for a little while."

He considers this for a moment. "Does this mean you're running away?"

"No, of course not. It means I'm taking a break. I'm an animal who likes to be outside occasionally. I need to keep up my hunting skills and I can't very well do that inside, can I?"

Chester looks around. "But this is mostly a parking lot. Except for those bushes. What are you going to hunt out here?"

He thinks he knows everything, but honestly, he doesn't. "There's a tree in the back that's full of birds I've had my eye on for weeks. I want to take a crack at some of those."

"I'm sorry, Franklin, but I'm thinking about how that will make Amelia and Connie feel. Amelia's having a hard time right now, and when they realize you're gone, they'll probably think you don't want to live here with them."

"I do want to live with them! I just want a little fresh air is all!"

"That's not what they'll think. It might make Amelia feel worse than she already does."

Oh boy, this dog sure knows how to make a cat feel bad. "What should I do?" I ask him.

Sara is at the car, opening the door for Gus. "Come on, Ches! Time to go!"

He starts toward her but thinks about it and turns back to me: "I would go back. I think you might be able to help Amelia through this bad patch she's having. I'm not sure how exactly, but I have a feeling you're the right pet for her right now."

Chester can be exasperating sometimes, the way he makes everything sound so simple. "I'd *like* to help, but I can't go to school with her and school is where all her *problems* are."

He nods the way dogs do, by pretending to sniff the air.

"You're right. It won't be easy. You'll have to think about it and find a way, but you're smart, Franklin—it'll come to you. I should go now."

It'll come to me! That's easy for him to say! He's a dog who can go anywhere with Gus as long as he's at the end of a leash. Cats can't deal with leashes or do anything like that.

But maybe he's right. Amelia and I are alike in many ways. We mean well but get in fights we regret afterward. I've made some friends, but it's not always easy for me.

Now that Amelia is having this bad spell, maybe I could try telling her my own stories about p intlessly fighting with other cats. I could remind her that sometimes friends don't look the way you expect them to. I could tell her that the two best friends I've ever had—Rocky and Chester—haven't even been cats, and maybe she should consider making friends with people who don't look like her at all.

I don't know if this will help, but I have to admit that Chester's got a good point: I could at least *try*.

I turn around to head back inside, only to realize that I might have a bigger problem: I look down at a long row of identical brown doors with bushes across from them and not much else. I can't remember which apartment is ours. Some doors have mats and potted flowers beside them, but I left too quickly to notice what ours had.

Think carefully, I tell myself.

I meow outside of one door and guess wrong. An old man opens it and tells me to scram or he'll call the superintendent.

The next door smells wrong to me, like spicy cooking, which Connie never does. After that, I get more frantic and try to retrace my steps. How far did I run to reach my bush? I can't even tell which bush I hid in because so many dogs have marked different spots. They all smell the same now—like the urine of strangers. There's nothing I can do except wait for Connie or Amelia to notice that I'm gone and come out to look for me.

Then I remember something: the tree outside Amelia's window! If I climb it, she'll be able to see me out here. The apartment is on the first floor, but I know from sitting in the window that you can see one branch clearly. I've had a great view of any bird who lands there. If I can get to that branch, Amelia will see me and know that I made a terrible mistake and I'm trying to get back inside again.

I follow a narrow line of grass around the building to the backyard. I know right away which tree is hers. The problem is, I can't seem to climb it. I'm a little out of shape and possibly heavier than I was last time I was outside. I don't know how this happened. All I do is eat what Amelia gives me and try to finish it before it gets stale.

One leap onto the tree trunk and I fall back to the ground. Another jump and one paw catches but the other doesn't. On the third try I'm ready, claws out. I get ahold of it and shimmy myself up to the lowest branch.

I wait and catch my breath. This isn't the branch closest to Amelia's window, though. I need to move across two more branches to reach that one. It's scary, for sure. Everything feels different up here. Things on the ground look small and the leaves look bigger than they should be. If a bird landed beside me on this branch, I don't know what I'd do. I've been watching them from so far away that a bird up close might look frightening, like the ancient dinosaurs I once saw on *The Land Before Time*, which I watched with Emily and regretted the minute I saw those birds. They scared me for a long time, the way they'll swoop in and eat anything.

I think about Amelia's cat video. Cats aren't supposed to be scared of much, but I'm not sure who decided that, because I'm scared of everything right now: of a bird landing, of a branch breaking, of a wolf sitting down at the bottom of this tree and waiting for me to fall on top of it.

I manage to move across one more branch, but I lose my footing and almost fall, which is enough to stop me from going any farther. I'm not where I need to be, but I can't move anymore and I don't know what to do. Now if Amelia looks for me outside her window, I won't be there. And if Connie opens the front door I won't be there either.

The worst part is another fact I'm remembering from Amelia's video but forgot until just now. Cats' claws only go one way, which means we can climb up trees but have a terrible time climbing down.

Why didn't I remember this?

I'm stuck. This is awful. Worse than the first time I was locked outside after Emily's family left. At least then I could move around and I had Genghis, who might have eaten all my food but also gave me tips for surviving on my own. What good will those tips do if I'm trapped in a tree that no one ever looks at except me?

I start meowing even though I know no one will hear me through the double-paned windows I've sat behind myself. My ears might be four times better than a person's, but even I can't hear what's happening out here.

Above me the sky darkens. The air grows cold. Apartment lights turn on as neighbors I've never seen return from work.

I don't know if I've ever felt so lonely and so scared.

Yes, I've been on my own before, but I was in better shape back then. Maybe it's only been a month or so, but it feels like much longer. Now I'm weighed down by many things, including worry about Amelia. I want to help her. Even if I can't solve all her problems, I certainly don't want to add to them by scaring her when she realizes I'm gone. I don't want her to think I ran away because I don't want to keep living here with her.

It's been hours and I don't understand why they haven't noticed me missing and come outside to look for me. The only explanation I can think of is that seeing Chester and Gus made Amelia worse and Connie's too worried to notice that I'm gone.

In the dark, I see evening animals start to creep out of their hiding spots. A skunk ambles below me with a walk that reminds me of Rocky. "Hello!" I call. "Up here! In the tree!"

He throws a look over his shoulder but doesn't stop walking. "No thanks," he says, even though I haven't asked him anything. "Cats attract coyotes. You're their favorite treat. I don't need that hassle."

Coyotes? It hadn't even occurred to me to worry about them. Now it has.

Above me, bats begin flying around on their evening bug hunt.

"Hello!" I call out to them. "Do any of you remember

me? I met a few of you when I was sleeping in a lawn mower shed."

They either don't remember me or are too busy to answer. I don't know why I'm calling out to strangers except that suddenly I feel lonelier than I ever have before.

Maybe this is what school is like for Amelia these days—surrounded by creatures who are so different from her, they won't even stop and say hello. It's a terrible feeling. I start to make a sound I don't even recognize. A wavery yowl, like a kitten that hasn't even opened its eyes. *What is that sound?* I think. And then I realize: this is what a crying cat sounds like.

CHAPTER TWENTY-ONE

I WAKE UP HOURS LATER TO A flashlight shining in my eyes.

"She was right. It *is* you. Come on down, Benjamin. Amelia's inside staring out her window and crying."

At long last! It's Connie! I've never been so grateful to see anyone, except I can't see her. The light shining in my eyes is too bright, but I can hear her voice.

I call back in my new plaintive voice that makes me sound much younger than I am. *I don't know how to get down*, I cry. *The branch is too thin to turn around and cats can't walk backward. At least not on little branches like this one.*

"Just jump, Benj. It's not as high as you think and Amelia's inside, hysterical."

I can't see the ground or anything else with this confusing

light in my eyes. I know cats are meant to be good jumpers, but I've gotten fat. I could break a leg or something worse. I think about Genghis and his stubby half tail. I don't think he lost it jumping out of a tree, but he might have. He's taken a lot of risks like this.

Then I think: Amelia needs me. I have to do it.

I fly off the branch, into the darkness. Connie's right. The ground is closer than I thought. I'm fine.

A second later, Connie picks me up and I'm better than fine. "Silly cat. You thought you were stuck up there and you weren't really. You just needed someone to point it out."

Inside, Amelia is sitting up in bed, holding out her arms. Connie hands me over and I can feel Amelia's tears in my fur and on my whiskers. She hugs me hard the way Emily used to, before her mother taught her to be gentle with me. I don't mind with Amelia. I purr to let her know that I never meant to run away and leave her for so long and I'll never do anything like that again. She lies back and tucks me under the covers with her.

"He thought he was stuck but he wasn't very high up in the tree. Poor cat. It's like he was trying to get back in through your window."

That's exactly what I was trying to do, I say after Connie turns out the light and leaves us alone.

In the dark, Amelia whispers, "I'm so glad you're back."

After the afternoon we've had, it's wonderful just to hear her talking again. I remember something Chester once said about Gus: The meltdowns are terrible, but they always end. He always comes back to being himself.

I am, too, I say.

The next morning, I wake up early and think about what I want to say to Amelia—the ideas I'd like to convey, even if she can't hear me perfectly. When she opens her eyes, I put one paw on her arm and say, *I think you and I have the same problem. We send the wrong message to people. You didn't mean to get angry at school. I didn't mean to run away.*

She doesn't answer, of course, but that's okay.

Being a cat means you make mistakes, socially. That's just how we are.

For the rest of the morning she stays in bed, not doing any of her usual things like reading or drawing or looking at cat books. She also doesn't say anything: no stories, no talking to herself in her singsong voice. It's unsettling to have so much quiet in the room.

To fill the silence, I tell her stories from my life where being catlike helped me survive. I tell her about Emily's family leaving me behind and how lonely it was, realizing the world was big and full of strangers. And then, one by one, I got to know a few. The bats, first. Then Rocky.

That's how it works, I say. *Eventually I figured out, my best friends weren't the ones I thought I'd have anything in common with. You have to give them a chance to surprise you. And maybe you'll surprise yourself.*

I keep going for a while and tell her about my adventures with Rocky. I'm not sure what my point is, but it's nice just to remember those times.

Chester is another example, I say. *I didn't think much of him in the beginning. We cats can be terrible snobs about dogs. To us, they seem silly, following commands and walking up and down the street at the end of a leash. But now I've learned they're not so silly. They've given themselves a hard job and they're good at what they do.*

Suddenly it feels like I've taken all this time getting to what I really want to say: *I wish I could help you at school the way Chester helps Gus. Unfortunately I can't. But I know that classroom full of kids was the scariest place I've ever been. I don't blame you for feeling overwhelmed by it. I don't think I can ever go back there.*

Even as I say this, I remember something Chester said about Gus: sometimes they think your voice is their own thoughts.

I wonder if this is true. If it is, maybe I shouldn't tell Amelia how scary school seemed to me. I should be saying: *School seemed okay! I distinctly remember one or two nice kids!*

I try an experiment. I say, *I think when you go back to school, you should consider spending more of your time with Chester and Gus. That way, Chester can look out for both of you. He's very good at that sort of thing. Probably better than I am, if you want to know the truth.*

It's not easy to admit this.

Cats like to think of themselves as the best at everything because usually we are. It's not just a feeling I have, it's a fact. I've seen the documentary.

After lunch, which Amelia doesn't eat, Connie comes into Amelia's room and tells her they need to talk about what happened at school. "I know this is hard, sweetheart, but it's important for us to understand—what made you get so mad at those girls? What did they say?"

"Shayna asked me where I bought my shoes and I said Target, and they both laughed."

"Why? What's so funny about that?"

"They said you don't buy *shoes* at Target."

"Why not?"

"I don't know."

Amelia rolls over. She doesn't want to talk about it anymore, but Connie keeps going. "Girls who are insecure can be very mean. I know they were your friends last year, but you need to put your effort into finding new friends. It's not good for you to be around them."

"There isn't anyone else. Soon-Yi hates me, too. The mathletes don't even say hi in the hall because they say I don't study enough."

Unfortunately, this is true. She doesn't study enough. But that's only because she doesn't like math. It's not really her fault.

Connie reaches over and squeezes Amelia's hand. I know Amelia doesn't like hugs. Hugs make her feel like she can't breathe, but hands don't breathe, so this is okay.

It must be, because she doesn't pull her hand away.

"It's possible this is always going to be hard for you, Am. Because other kids do and say confusing things. It's easy to get mad, but I don't think you like getting mad. I think you want to have friends and maybe you need some help figuring out how to do that. Maybe that guidance counselor, Ms. Pitts, can help. She might have good ideas on who you can be friends with."

You could be friends with Gus, I whisper. I try not to say anything when Connie is talking—in case Amelia can hear me, I don't want to confuse her with too many voices at once. But this feels like an important suggestion to make. *Then you can hang out with him and Chester. I don't think they're so busy at recess and lunch.*

Amelia doesn't say anything. She pulls her hand away to let Connie know she's done talking.

CHAPTER TWENTY-TWO

THE NEXT MORNING, JACK, AMELIA'S DAD,
stops by. He looks a little frantic, like he might have slept in
the clothes he's wearing and he definitely hasn't brushed his
hair in a long time.

"Hi, Kitty Cat," he says, which I assume means he's talking to me, except he's looking at Amelia.

"Hi, Dad."

"I'm sorry I missed last Saturday. You wouldn't believe
how crazy work is. I honest-to-God thought it was Friday."

He waits for a while but Amelia doesn't say anything.

"Okay. So." He looks down at a paper bag in his hands.
"I brought you a present." He reaches into the bag and pulls
out a stuffed tiger. Even though it doesn't look anything

like a real tiger, he says, "It's Rajah. I stopped by the zoo gift shop."

Even though Amelia isn't talking, I can guess what she's thinking: *That's not Rajah.*

Amelia loves Rajah because he's big and powerful and makes his own rules. Yes, he's stuck in a zoo, but he gets to decide which animals he's stuck with. If it was possible, Amelia would like to do the same thing herself. She'd like to be so powerful that she could pick the other children in her classroom, and then she would only choose the ones who are nice to her because, maybe, they're a little scared of her. She's never said this out loud, of course. It's a theory I have because I think Amelia and I have a lot in common and any time she talks about Rajah, this is how I feel.

I also know this: Amelia doesn't like stuffed animals. Toys like this make her mad because she doesn't like playing pretend. That's why it wasn't fun to go over to Maura's and Shayna's houses when they wanted to act out stories she'd never read where some people are witches and others are wizards and none of it is real.

A stuffed Rajah isn't exactly like that, but it's close. It's not real. It's not powerful like Rajah and it's definitely not in control.

"Okay, so I'll leave him here, all right?" Jack says, putting the toy tiger down on the bed near her feet.

Amelia obviously doesn't want to talk to him, but he can't leave if it's only been two minutes since he got here. He starts moving around the room, picking up random papers and putting them back down. He finds her math study guide and flips through it.

"Your mom had an idea that maybe I could help you study for the Math Olympiad. What do you think?"

Sometimes I feel like I might know Amelia better than her parents. I wish they would watch her and realize: she likes drawing. In fact, that's all she does. Since Amelia still isn't talking, I say: *I think it's a little late for that. Plus, she's not a huge fan of math.*h

Jack holds up a math worksheet he's found on her desk. "Like here, on this ratio problem. You needed to divide, not subtract." He pulls a pen out of his pocket and corrects it. "Easy mistake. I'd be happy to work on this with you."

He keeps looking through her study guides for a while, making corrections and notes in the margins. When he's finally done, he says, "You're missing a lot on geometry and fractions, but you're doing okay on the other parts."

I think this is his idea of being nice.

He stands up like he's about to leave, and then sits back down. "Look, Amelia, I know you're upset that Sandy and I are moving in together. I understand she's not your favorite person in the world because she didn't love seeing Rajah the same way you do. But I think you need to give her a chance, okay? I love you both. I really do."

I wait to see what Amelia will say. He seems like he's at least trying to be nice and maybe she should try to be nice, too.

We all wait. I think we're all holding our breath. Or maybe it's just me, I'm not sure.

Eventually he says, "Okay then. I'll see you later, I guess," and leaves.

For a little while, Amelia doesn't move. Then after we hear the front door open and close, Amelia reaches down, picks up the stuffed Rajah, and wraps her arms around it so tight it would have had a hard time breathing if it were alive and needed to.

I remember Chester telling me once that you have to watch your person carefully and look for clues. To me, this is a clue: I think it means she either 1) doesn't hate her dad or 2) she really misses Rajah or 3) both.

CHAPTER TWENTY-THREE

"I'VE JUST TALKED TO MS. PITTS," Connie says that afternoon. I can tell she's trying to sound cheerful, but she also looks like she hasn't been sleeping much.

It's been hard. Amelia gets out of bed to go to the bathroom but not much else. She eats a few bites from plates of food that Connie leaves for her. Sometimes I eat a little just to remind Amelia how eating works.

I'm not sure how effective this is. After I've taken a few bites of her food, Amelia never eats any more of it.

I've heard Connie on the phone saying this episode seems worse than anything she's seen before. She doesn't want to push her too much. She wants to give her space, but she also doesn't want this to go on for too long.

"We both agree that you shouldn't go back to school until

you're feeling better. I told her I would homeschool you for a little while, so you can keep up. Of course I won't be great at the math stuff, but maybe we can ask for your dad's help. How does that sound?"

Amelia doesn't answer.

Great! I say.

I didn't know there was such a thing as going to school at home. To me it sounds perfect. No cafeteria to worry about. No recess. No roomful of noisy kids. I wonder what subjects we'll learn. Chester says science is his favorite. He also likes social studies, but I'm not sure what that means, unless it's about social skills, which I probably won't be very good at.

Amelia doesn't say anything to her mom's suggestion. I move closer to her on the bed to make sure she's not sleeping through this announcement. She's not. Her eyes are open.

When we're alone again, I stretch out beside Amelia. *I like this homeschooling idea.*

It means I can learn the same things you do. Chester's good at being surrounded by children but I might be a better student. I don't want to brag, but I believe I'm interested in a wider range of topics than he is.

I certainly wouldn't fall asleep if there's an interesting lesson being taught, which he admitted he sometimes does. I also wouldn't have passed up on the chance to learn how to read the way he did. He told me the story of how his old trainer made flash cards with commands written on them so he could prove he was reading.

"Were you?" I asked him.

"I don't think so. I recognized a few letters and memorized the cards. 'Sit' was easy. That's short. Three letters. 'Roll over' is more letters. You do it that way."

I didn't say this to him, but I do wonder if dogs limit their potential by getting all caught up in obeying commands. If you never start doing that, maybe someone will teach you to read something more interesting than sit and roll over.

It doesn't take long to figure out that you can't do much homeschooling with a person who doesn't want to do any schoolwork.

After a few stabs, Connie gives up on the assignments the teacher has sent home and starts reading aloud. Most of the books she chooses are about cats, which is nice of her. My favorite is about a cat named Jenny Linsky, who lives in New York and tries to befriend a group of neighborhood cats who meet under the same sycamore tree every night. It's hard, though, because she's new and none of them will talk to her. So Jenny goes off and teaches herself how to ice skate at the local rink to impress them. It works. When they see her, they all applaud and want to learn to skate themselves.

It's not a very realistic story. In my experience, cats don't ice skate and they never meet up in groups like that.

In the next story, Jenny's good enough friends with the other cats to go out for a night of dancing but she doesn't know the latest dance moves and feels too shy to join. Eventually she gets the idea to show the others her favorite dance, which they all love and ask her to teach them.

Again, this isn't very realistic. Cats don't dance. We'd look silly if we tried, and we hate looking silly.

I get the feeling Connie is reading these stories because they're about a cat having a hard time making friends. The message of each one seems to be: be yourself. This is nice, of course, except it doesn't always work. When Amelia is herself and talks about the things that interest her, the other kids tell her she's going on too long or doing something else wrong.

After another day of silence, Connie tries a different approach: she tells Amelia she's been on the phone with her teacher, Ms. Winger. "She says if you're going to stay home, you have to do something, but you have a choice. You can read the same book as the class or you can start a journal. If you choose the journal, you have to write in it every day."

I think about her sketchbook, which she hasn't opened since her last day at school. I say softly, *You should pick the journal. Then you can draw in it.*

Amelia doesn't say anything, but Connie leans closer and asks again. "Do you want to read the book with the class?"

"No," she says.

"Or keep a journal?"

I don't know if Connie feels the same way I do—that we'd trade fast talking for silence if we could. I suspect she would.

"Yes," Amelia says.

That afternoon, Connie brings her a new notebook. "Here it is, Am. Ms. Pitts says it might help you sort out your feelings if you write about them."

It's hard to imagine Amelia writing about her feelings, but she must have an idea for something to write about because after Connie leaves the journal on her bed, she sits up in bed and opens the cover. She runs her hand over the blank pages and then, for the first time in days, she gets out of bed for something other than the bathroom. She brings her journal to her desk, where she finds a pencil and a ruler that she uses to draw a thick line down the center of the first page, then three lines across. Her face has a new expression on it: concentrated, focused. At this point, she's only drawn a bunch of boxes, but she must have an idea.

I step closer to see what she's going to put in them, but she moves her arm so I can't see.

Whatever the idea is, she gets to work right away. I remember her once telling me about books where the stories are mostly pictures, but they're not for little kids. "They're called graphic novels," she said. "The pictures are in blocks across the page like comics. If they're good, they can tell a whole story with very few words. Just pictures. You fill in the words yourself."

I wonder if that's what she's doing now. Maybe she wants to tell her side of the story about what happened at school in a way that all of us can understand. I know it wasn't just about those girls laughing at her shoes. Maybe she can explain to her mom in pictures why school is so hard for her these days.

CHAPTER TWENTY-FOUR

FOR THE NEXT DAY, NOTHING CHANGES, except for little things. Connie convinces Amelia to come to the table to eat, which is nice. She still isn't talking much, but it's a little progress. Enough that Connie says okay when Ms. Pitts, the guidance counselor at school, asks if she can stop by for a visit. Once Connie hangs up the phone, though, she worries. I can tell by the way she starts cleaning the living room, shoving the open, half-unpacked boxes that I've been enjoying and sleeping in on a regular basis into her bedroom.

I wouldn't worry about that, I try to tell her. *Some people like messes.* I know she can't hear me, but still it feels important to remind her: *Better to focus on getting Amelia cleaned up.*

One thing Amelia won't do now that she's home all the

time is take a shower. She's always hated showers because the water hurts her skin and if she accidentally bumps the handle, it gets way too hot and *really* hurts.

To me, this seems reasonable. As a cat, I might enjoy watching water, but I certainly don't like getting wet. Rainy days were the worst part of living on my own. Get caught in a storm and you can't think straight as you fly around in a panic looking for cover anywhere. That's how you find yourself spending a whole day under a car breathing in fumes and staring at pavement. I never understood why people not only create a rainstorm in their bathroom but take off all their clothes to stand in it. I can't believe more people don't refuse such unpleasantness.

Cats hate showers, I told Amelia the first time we talked about showers. *We don't understand why people bother when you can get perfectly clean in other ways.*

Now she hasn't showered in more than a week. I like the way she smells, but I also liked sleeping with my face in Marc's smelly running shoes. Chester was the one who told me this was a strange thing to do.

"Really?" I said. "You don't like that smell?"

"I don't mind it, but most people hate it. Sara usually tells Marc to leave his stinky shoes outside."

Amelia smells a lot like Marc's shoes at this point. I know

Connie has noticed because I saw her make a face when Amelia came to the table to eat. I suspect she hasn't said anything because Amelia has so many other problems at the moment, but if Ms. Pitts is coming over, she has to do something.

While Amelia is in the bathroom, she opens the door a crack. "While you're in there, Am, I have to tell you something. Ms. Pitts from school is coming over this afternoon. We don't really have a choice; she needs to check up on you. I think we should show her that you're doing okay. If we get you all cleaned up and put on fresh clothes, that's what she'll think."

Cats might hate the idea of taking a shower, but we're big ones for cleaning ourselves during a crisis. I tell Amelia, *This is a good idea. Washing up makes you look like you're not worried.* There's a long silence from the bathroom, so I add: *And then afterward, you're clean. Which makes you feel better.*

Still no response.

Finally Amelia opens the door. "No," she says, and moves past Connie back into her room. She slams the door shut before even I can follow her.

"I have to apologize," Connie says when Ms. Pitts arrives. "I don't think Amelia will be able to join us."

Ms. Pitts doesn't look too upset. "I'd love to see her if I can, but if not, that's okay. This will give us a chance to talk privately."

I don't know if "talk privately" means I'm supposed to leave the room, but I don't.

Ms. Pitts is very pretty, with a glamorous scarf and long, sparkly earrings that I have a hard time not staring at. Part of me would like to sit in her lap and bat at those earrings to see if they'll make a noise or sparkle more. Another part of me realizes I probably shouldn't do that.

"Let me tell you why I came," Ms. Pitts says. "We've been trying to figure out how we can help Amelia ease her way back into school. We're wondering what you'd think about having her come back for a short part of the school day. Just for one or two activities that we know she enjoys and is successful with."

Art class? I think. *Great idea!*

"I don't know," Connie says.

"Maybe she could start by returning for Math Olympiad practices? One of the mathletes has tested positive for mono, which means their team is short two members if Amelia doesn't return either. They're very eager to have her back and we know how good she is at math."

166

It's not a great idea! I shout at Connie. *She doesn't love math!*
She likes art!

"I don't think so," Connie says. "I have to tell you, the morning before her episode at school, Amelia begged me to let her stay home. She knew something bad was going to happen. I keep thinking about that and how I've pushed her because I've been listening to doctors instead of listening to *her.* I want to try doing things differently this time. I want *her* to tell me when she's ready to go back. I want her to know that we're listening to what she says and she does have some control over her life."

Ms. Pitts's eyebrows go up, which Chester told me is a sign that someone is either surprised or scared. "A lot of children might say they don't want to go to school."

"I understand that, but it's different with Amelia. School has been so demoralizing for her this year. I want her to rebuild some of her self-confidence before she goes back. I don't think she can do that when she's around other kids."

"I'd say learning how to be around other kids is an important part of building her self-esteem. She'll have to go back sooner or later. The longer she stays at home, the harder that might be."

Connie looks down. I suspect it's hard for her to argue

with someone who is a professional and also has sparkly, distracting earrings.

Ms. Pitts keeps going. "In our experience, when these incidents happen, it's best when kids come back as quickly as possible and make reparations. She can apologize to the other student, but more importantly, she can show the other students she's still the smart, capable, thoughtful girl they know and remember."

Connie takes a deep breath. "There's a bit more that I haven't told you. Amelia's been seeing a psychiatrist to deal with her anxiety. He thinks there might be more going on. When he saw her after this incident at school, he recommended taking her to a neurologist to have her screened for autism."

Ms. Pitts doesn't seem surprised by this. Her eyebrows stay right where they were. "I've wondered about that. There's been some new research recently that autism gets missed in girls, especially smart ones like Amelia whose passions aren't too out of the ordinary. Lots of girls love cats and animals. She also does a pretty good job of compensating. She can seem okay in certain social situations, until suddenly she's not and she's acting out in scary ways." She pulls a notebook out of her purse. "I imagine by now you've probably read the checklists. What did you think?"

Connie sighs. "She definitely has sensory issues. She can't stand taking showers."

Now I'm surprised. *Hating showers is a sign of autism?* I don't understand. Getting pelted by water drops is very unpleasant.

"She also won't eat food that has touched any other food."

This also seems wrong when anyone can tell you: mixing crunchy and soft is confusing for the mouth.

"At school she says she can't tell the difference when other kids are making fun of her or are just trying to be funny."

Doesn't everyone get confused by this? Cats certainly do. It's why we get in so many fights.

Ms. Pitts writes more notes. "Let me ask you—have you talked with Amelia about this?"

"I tried to after we saw the doctor, but she made it clear: she doesn't want another label. She doesn't want to be different than everyone else. I think she feels ashamed more than anything else."

Ashamed? Why should Amelia feel ashamed when apparently being autistic just means you act like a cat? Honestly, I see nothing wrong with any of these "signs" Connie has mentioned.

"I understand, but I think an honest conversation might be helpful. For some girls, getting diagnosed can be a big relief.

It explains some of the challenges they've never understood. For everyone else, socializing seems easy. For them, it isn't."

"I don't think it'll be a relief for her. She's had to make so many transitions this year. Her father and I separating, moving to this apartment—I'm afraid it'll be too much for her. She'll feel like a freak."

"It doesn't mean that at all."

"No, I agree. But I don't think that Amelia will feel that way."

They keep talking for a while. Ms. Pitts mentions a social skills group that meets with her at lunchtime once a week, where kids learn how to ask each other questions and listen with empathy. I'm not sure what empathy means, but I feel sorry for Connie, who has to say, "Yes, I know Amelia needs help with all those things. She wants to have friends, but she doesn't really understand how to *be* a friend."

I rub Connie's ankle to say, *Yes she does! She's a great friend to me!*

In the end it seems like Connie and Ms. Pitts agree on a lot of things except this: Connie still thinks it's too soon for Amelia to go back to school. "I have to trust my instincts on this. Right now they say it's not a good idea."

After Ms. Pitts leaves, I go back up the hall to Amelia's room and see that the door that she slammed shut is now open. I don't know if Connie will notice this, but I do. Did Amelia hear what they were talking about? Is she upset?

I walk in and she's in the same place she's been in for a few days: back at her desk, working on her graphic novel. I jump up on the bed beside her: *I don't know if you heard what they were saying, but if you did, you shouldn't worry about it. Being autistic is nothing to be ashamed of.*

Of course I know there's more to it than this. Even Connie admitted that Amelia doesn't have friends because she doesn't know how to be a friend. *I'm bad at all this social stuff, too. I never ask other animals questions. Because I don't really care about the answers. I've never seen the point. It's only recently that I've realized that having friends helps and if you want to have friends you have to be a friend. Chester taught me that, which sounds crazy, I know.*

I peek over from the bed and try to see what she's drawing. From what I can tell, it doesn't seem like her story is set in school. I don't see any people at all, just trees and sky, which makes me wonder if maybe she's not writing about her old friends at all. Maybe she's making up a new world she'd like to live in, something like Rajah's domain.

CHAPTER TWENTY-FIVE

CONNIE MUST BE THINKING ABOUT WHAT Ms. Pitts said, because the next day she calls Sara and invites her and Gus to come back. "Amelia's not ready to go back to school quite yet, but I'm hoping that seeing a friend from school might help her a little."

I can tell Amelia is excited when she hears this, but for some reason, she doesn't want her mom to know that she likes this idea. She's bent over at her desk, working on her book. She smiles but doesn't turn around or let her mother see.

I don't know if she's more excited to see Chester or Gus, but maybe it doesn't matter because Connie has a trick up her sleeve: "Before they come, you'll need to wash your hair, though. We can do it in the sink if you want, and you can take a sponge bath afterward."

Amelia doesn't answer. She's thinking about this. Trying to decide if one thing is worth the other.

Finally she nods, which makes Connie smile.

Saturdays are always noisy around here. Kids in neighboring apartments are home, along with their parents. TVs are on and some people play music with their windows open, which makes Amelia pace back and forth. She's already nervous about the visit from Chester and Gus and about the hair washing beforehand. She doesn't need any extra, confusing noise she can't control.

I circle her ankle, hoping she'll pick me up and sit with me in her lap, which might calm her. She does and it works. We sit for a while, scratching and purring.

"Amelia!" Connie calls from the kitchen. "Time to do your hair!"

She carries me into the other room like she's hoping maybe I'll take a turn getting my fur washed, which isn't going to happen, obviously. I'd like to help Amelia, but I don't see how getting my fur wet will do that.

I feel her heartbeat going a mile a minute as she steps toward the sink. I think: *She hates this as much as I would, only she has to do it.*

"Maybe if we cut your hair short this wouldn't be so hard?" Connie offers.

Amelia likes her curly bush of hair and being able to hide behind it. I like it, too. She shakes her head no and bends over, eyes shut. The shampoo in her eyes is the worst part. It hurts, I can tell. She wants to say something, but can't because then it'll go in her mouth, too.

The whole time, Connie whispers reassurances. "That's good . . . you're doing great . . . your hair will feel so good after this." After a long time rinsing, she finally says, "That's it! You're done!"

Amelia stands up, head dripping.

"Do you want to sit on the sofa for a minute and let Benj play with your wet curls? He likes that."

It's true, I do. And Amelia doesn't mind.

Connie fills the sink in the bathroom so Amelia can give the rest of herself a sponge bath. All these things take longer than they used to. It's hard to imagine this new Amelia getting ready in time for the school bus in the morning.

"Don't take too long," Connie says. "They'll be here in an hour."

Just then, the doorbell rings. Connie looks nervous. "That can't be them. It's an hour early." Amelia hasn't washed yet. She doesn't know what to do. She can't send them away again when she invited them this time.

"Why don't you go back to your room and get dressed? Don't worry about washing up for now."

I follow Connie into the living room. I need as much time as possible to tell Chester this whole story and get his suggestions. Mostly I want to hear what he thinks: Is school too hard for Amelia to manage or is Ms. Pitts right—should she go back and learn how to deal with it?

Connie opens the door, except it's not Chester and his family, it's Jack. He's holding a manila envelope in his hands. "I'm sorry I didn't call before I came, but I think I might have found a breakthrough for Amelia."

A breakthrough? I think. *Hooray!* Maybe Connie is thinking the same thing, because she steps away from the door and lets him in.

"I found my old study guides for the Math Olympiad. Do you remember how I was disqualified from competing with the team the first year but I went anyway? Apparently I took notes on every question they asked to share with the team later. I forgot I did that, but it's really quite useful."

"Oh, Jack, now isn't a good time. We're expecting some friends soon."

He looks surprised. "Friends? What friends?"

"Friends from school. The ones who gave us the cat."

"What cat?"

Connie looks surprised. "Amelia's new cat. Didn't you see him when you were here before? He was in her room with her."

"I didn't see any cat."

If Jack didn't notice me when I was lying on the bed next to Amelia while he talked to her, it makes me wonder what else he hasn't noticed.

He looks down at me. "Oh, right. You have a cat now."

"His name is Benjamin Franklin and he's been wonderful with Amelia. A huge help through this whole hard time she's having."

"Okay," he says, holding up the envelope. "So can I just leave this with her? It'll only take a minute."

There's not much Connie can do to stop him. He goes to Amelia's room and opens the door. "I brought you something, Amelia. I can't stay long, but I thought—"

He stops talking. I follow him in and look around. Amelia isn't here.

"Amelia? Are you in the bathroom?'

The door across the hall is closed.

We wait for a long time and finally she calls out from the bathroom, "Can you leave whatever you brought on the desk? I can't talk right now."

I'm relieved. She's taking her sponge bath, getting herself ready to see Chester and Gus. It's a good sign. I don't want her dad's arrival to mess this up. I follow him over to her desk, where he drops the envelope. He stops when he sees her sketchbook there.

You shouldn't look at that, I say. *She's not letting anyone see it.*

"Huh," he says, and opens it up.

He flips through a few pages, looks back at the door, and flips through a few more. I jump up on the desk to stop him. It's possible this is a story about him. I think about all the Rajah pictures she's drawn. Maybe this is a story where Rajah shows his love for Amelia by breaking out of his domain and eating her dad.

I mean it, I tell him, moving onto the desk and putting out a paw to stop him. *You really shouldn't look at that.*

That's when I see something surprising. It's not a drawing of Rajah, it's a picture of *me*. I take my paw away and he turns a page. In the first box is a drawing of leaves and beyond them, a skunk, from the point of view of someone up in a tree. You can see the two perfect stripes on his back. It's a great drawing, except I don't understand: Amelia was never up in a tree, looking down on a skunk.

I was.

My heart speeds up. I look at the next panel. Same

viewpoint, only this time there are more leaves and bats, flying around beyond them. I'm not in the picture, I'm *seeing* it.

How did she do this? How did she know what I saw when I was alone in the tree on the night I escaped?

And then, all at once, I remember: I told her. That night, when I finally got inside, I told her everything. The bats who wouldn't help me, the skunk who tried to scare me.

Amelia heard my whole story! She *can* hear me!

Jack shakes his head and flips another page. "She's pretty good," he says quietly. He turns to me. "I can see why you like it. It's all about you."

Just then, there's a sound in the doorway. "Don't look at that," Amelia says.

I jump off the desk and Jack steps away.

"I'm sorry, Am. I know I shouldn't look at your private things, but it's good. You're a very good artist. Or cartoonist. Whatever this is called."

"It's a graphic novel."

"Okay. Well, it's good."

"It's not finished. I don't want anyone to see it until it's done."

"Fine. I'm sorry. But maybe you don't have to be quite so defensive when someone is paying you a compliment.

You're a very good artist, Am. That's all I wanted to say."

In a way, he's right, he just hasn't said it very nicely. Amelia looks confused. "What are you doing here, Dad? I'm getting ready to see some friends from school."

"Oh yeah." He looks back at the envelope on the desk. "I wanted to bring you this. I found an old study guide for the Math Olympiad from the year I was disqualified. Because I couldn't compete, I went and wrote down all the questions they asked, along with the answers. I thought it might be helpful."

"Why were you disqualified?"

"I'd had—well, a disagreement with my teammates. They thought I overreacted when other people made mistakes. They were worried because they said judges take off points for unsportsmanlike conduct so they banded together and voted me off the team."

Amelia looks surprised. I can tell by her eyebrows. "*Really?*"

"Yeah, it was pretty embarrassing actually. But it made me realize that I needed to make some changes. Learn to control my temper."

He doesn't seem to realize that Amelia might find this story helpful. That there might be some parallels between his behavior and hers. But then, he didn't notice that Amelia has a cat now either. I guess obvious things escape him.

Amelia looks at the ground. "I've gotten mad at math practice, too. Only usually I'm the one making mistakes and then I scream at everyone else and tell them not to get so mad at me."

"Yeah, well—if you want to know the truth, I never saw a judge take off any points for poor conduct. I think it's something coaches just say to scare people."

Amelia looks away. "Still. It's probably not good to get so mad."

I'm glad she can see this, even if her dad can't.

"No, you're right. That's why I went to the competition and took all these notes. I was trying to do something nice to help my teammates and also apologize to them."

"Did it work?"

"Yes, as a matter of fact. They let me back on the team the next year and some of them eventually became my best friends."

This is the part of the story she's heard a lot—how he met his best friends on the Math Olympiad team. I don't think she's ever heard the earlier part.

She looks down. She's still wearing a bathrobe, not clothes. "I can't really talk now, Dad. I should get ready."

"Sure, sure. I understand. Have a nice time with your friend and take a look at that study guide. If you have any questions, I'll be happy to stop by again and go over it with you."

After he's gone, I jump up on the bed and ask her, "Did you really make your whole book about me?"

She doesn't answer.

I don't understand. If she can't hear me, how did she know I was up in the tree? How did she draw *exactly* what I saw?

I don't have the answer yet, but I can't wait to tell Chester and find out what he thinks.

The doorbell rings. Amelia is shy when we get to the living room. I know she's nervous about seeing Gus again. One of the main things Amelia's learned this year is how easy it is to say the wrong thing. Afterward, it's always impossible to explain. She only says what she's thinking. Doesn't everyone do this? But her thoughts come out the wrong way. They hurt people's feelings. "You don't want people to think you're a bully, do you?" Ms. Winger once said.

She doesn't. Amelia hates bullies and doesn't understand how she could so often be mistaken for one.

I suspect this is what has kept her so quiet recently.

I think Amelia wants to talk again—really talk, the way she used to—but she's scared. Gus is good practice because he's not good at talking either and Chester is there and she loves Chester. Still, she's nervous. So am I.

Gus and Sara are already sitting on the sofa when we walk in. Connie is sitting in a chair across from them with her hands on her lap. They all look awkward, like maybe they haven't said anything at all while they were waiting for us.

"Here they are!" Connie says. "Amelia and Benjamin!"

Chester sits up. "They still haven't figured out your real name?" he says to me.

"No, but it's okay. We've had a very enlightening few days."

"Amelia looks better."

"Well, she cleaned herself up at least. She still isn't saying much, but the good news is that I think I might have figured out the problem."

"What?"

"She doesn't like saying the wrong things and it happens a lot."

"That makes sense." He doesn't say any more because figuring out the problem isn't the same thing as solving it. "How are you doing? I'm sorry I couldn't help you more on our last visit."

"I'm fine. I might be even better than fine. I have some new proof that Amelia might understand what I've been saying to her."

"Really?"

"She's been working on a book lately instead of going to school. It turns out the book is all about me!"

No cat likes to openly brag. We'd rather sit quietly and have other people point out our achievements. Even saying this much makes me self-conscious, but Chester is my friend. I'm hoping he'll understand.

"I was very surprised. It includes details I've only mentioned in passing, but it means she's *heard* them, right?"

"Yes, definitely. That's wonderful, Franklin."

I wonder if Chester would like Gus to make a book about him. All of a sudden, I feel bad. "How is Gus doing?"

"Mostly good. He uses his talking computer at school a little more these days. Sometimes he even uses it with other kids, which is nice to see."

"Does he ever use it with you?"

"No. I usually know what he's thinking, so he doesn't need to."

"How do you think that happened? That he started understanding you?"

"I'm not sure. I think when you're a pet with a job like ours, you watch your person so much that you start to think like them. They can understand you because you understand them."

He's right about one thing. I didn't understand much

183

about Amelia when I first got here. Now I do.

Above us, I hear Connie saying my name. "We're so grateful for Benjamin. He's such a good, funny cat. At dinnertime, he sometimes sits in the empty chair."

I hope hearing this doesn't make Chester wish he was a cat who could sit at the dinner table with his family.

Connie keeps going: "The important thing is, he's been wonderful for Amelia. It's strange to realize he's only been with us for less than a month. It feels like much longer. I can't imagine life without him."

"I'm not that great," I reassure Chester. "I still haven't figured out a way to get Amelia to go back to school. I think she should, but I'm not sure. If she's at school, I won't be with her. That's the problem. There's a limit on what service cats can do."

Chester gives me a funny look.

"What?" I say.

"Nothing. I've just never heard of a service cat before. I like it. I think it fits. Technically, you haven't been through the training, but that's okay."

"What training?"

"Service dogs spend the first two years of their life getting ready. We live with a trainer for a year or sometimes two and we learn everything we need to know."

I didn't know this. "What did you learn?"

"They have to teach you a lot of things because you don't know who your person will be yet. You might work for a blind person or you might work for someone in a wheelchair whose hands don't work well. You have to learn about cars and traffic, but you also have to learn a lot of vocabulary words of things you might need to fetch, like car keys or wallet or cell phone."

This is all news to me. I certainly know what those things are, but I can't picture myself dragging any of them across the room.

"But you don't fetch those things."

That's when he looks sad and tells me something I've never known. "Technically, I didn't pass my service dog training. I was too sound sensitive. There was some thunder during my test and I wasn't able to stay on task."

"*Thunder?* While you were being *tested*?" It's unimaginable. I don't know any animal who isn't scared of thunder. "What did you do?"

He looks away sheepishly. "I ran away and hid."

"Of course you did, Ches! Any sensible animal would. You can die from thunder unless you hide."

"Actually, that's not true. It just feels that way to us. Thunder is loud, that's all. It can't hurt you."

"It *can't*?" This is very surprising to me. It doesn't sound right.

"No. I've looked into it and watched the Weather Channel so I can learn more. Lightning can hurt you but it's very rare and almost never hurts animals, only tall things like trees."

"So if you failed your test, and you're not a service dog, what are you exactly?"

"I'm a therapy dog with a special certification in seizure response."

"Huh. What does that mean?"

"It means I get to know Gus very well. I watch him for clues other people don't see. I anticipate what's coming and I look for solutions."

"That's what I'm trying to do!"

"It's not easy."

"No, it isn't."

We haven't been following the mothers' conversation for a while, but suddenly people are standing. Amelia is going to show Gus her bedroom, apparently. Chester stands up, too, but I'm surprised. Sara hands Gus his talking board and sits back down.

"You two go on," Sara says. "See if the animals want to go with you."

Connie sits, too, and suddenly it's the four of us walking up the hallway.

I feel proud of Amelia. An hour ago she was hiding in the bathroom when her dad came into her room. Now she's okay with it. Quiet, but okay.

She opens the door and we all walk in.

Gus squeals and flaps his hands a little. For the first time, I see Amelia do her toe bouncing in front of someone else. She makes a sound like a squeak that might be a giggle, it's hard to tell. Gus rocks and laughs when he sees the cat pictures.

It's strange. For a little while, the pets are the stillest things in the room.

The moms might have pretended they weren't going to follow us, but now they're standing out in the hallway, whispering to themselves. I'm not sure what they're talking about because I'm too busy watching Gus and Amelia.

Amelia touches Gus's talking board. He gets it to make a funny squeaking sound. She laughs and tries to find the button to make the sound herself.

Me, I don't care for the sound.

By my third time hearing it, my ears twitch to get away. I look over at Chester. He's trying to pretend he doesn't mind it either, but this is my friend. I know he doesn't like it.

"He found a program that does sound effects," Chester says. His voice sounds strained. "This one is a firecracker exploding. I've told him it's not my favorite sound in the world. But I've gotten used to it. Nothing really explodes. It's just a sound."

I turn and look at him, with admiration. He's trained himself not to be scared of these sounds because he doesn't want to leave a room where Gus might need him.

I want to be as brave as he is.

Amelia asks for another sound by tapping his talking board. She doesn't use any words, but Gus knows what she's saying. Gus taps a button and the sound of birds fills the room. At first, my ears think they're real birds and I get excited, but of course birds don't fly through windows that are shut and have screens on them.

I look back at the moms in the hall. I wonder if this is the first time Connie has seen Amelia do some of these things, like bounce on her toes and flap her hands. She looks confused, like maybe it is. But I also know this is the first time either one of us has seen Amelia smile since her incident at school.

Sara is smiling, too. I think it's because Gus is having something close to a conversation. He and Amelia are taking turns pressing sounds on his board. With each new sound, they smile. Even if it's not funny—like a jackhammer on the streets or an ambulance siren—they laugh at the surprise.

Here's what I notice: with Gus, *not talking* makes it easier to communicate. For the first time, Amelia isn't saying the wrong thing. They are playing a different way. Taking turns and laughing. "I've never seen Gus do this before," I whisper to Chester.

"Neither have I," he says, which makes me feel good, like Amelia has accomplished something important.

"Did they do this at school?"

"Not that I saw. Usually when they sat together, Amelia talked to me. But toward the end, I started to get the feeling that Gus was listening to what she said."

"What did she talk to you about?"

"Her troubles with the other girls and making friends in general. She had a lot of trouble with that."

"Ms. Pitts and Connie do think Amelia might have autism."

Chester puts his nose in the air. "Yeah, I've been thinking that for a while."

"Why didn't you *tell* me? You already said you're not a neurologist!"

"I don't love labels. I think pets should get to know their person without them. The most important thing to remember about autism is that it isn't bad. It's just different."

"Amelia doesn't want to be different."

"Maybe that's what you can help her with."

Amelia sits down on the bed and bounces a few times. I've seen this before, but always when we're alone. Gus sits down on the other side of the bed and does the same thing. They both bounce and laugh.

Watching this from the hallway, the moms smile.

"She does seem better," Chester says.

"Let me ask you this question," I say. "Connie is happy having Amelia at home, where she's less stressed and seems happier, but Ms. Pitts thinks Amelia should go back to school as soon as possible. She says the longer Amelia stays away, the harder it'll be for her to go back."

"What do you think?" Chester asks.

"I don't *know*. That's why I'm asking you."

"What does she do all day at home?"

I think about the different ways I might answer this question. How the first few days, I would have had to say "nothing," but this week is different. I tell him how hard she's been working on her graphic novel.

"Oh, right. The book about you."

"I don't know if it's all about me. I only saw a page or two about the last time you visited when I got locked outside for most of the night and other animals told me it wasn't safe

190

for me to be there. I think maybe they were having a joke at my expense. It's hard for me to tell with other animals. I can't really read them."

"When it's hard to read people, it's easy to assume they're being mean. I think that happened with Amelia."

"I've heard the stories, Ches. Sometimes they *were* mean."

"I know. But sometimes they weren't. And sometimes she was mean, too. I wonder if she's trying to say something with this book. You stopped going outside for a while and then when you finally did, it was scary. But if she's thinking about that and drawing it, maybe it means she'd like to go back to school."

It's hard for me to imagine why I ever thought Chester was a dopey dog. He's the opposite, really. He's the smartest animal I know.

"I think you're right, Chester."

His nose goes up again, but he's only pretending to sniff. Really, he's smiling, I can tell.

"It means you're helping her even when you might not realize it. I wouldn't worry about her not answering when you talk to her. I think some people hear us but don't let themselves believe it because that would mean they're different and they don't want to be. Most people can't hear their pets and they want to be like other people."

Right then, Gus squeals and stands up from the bed. His talking computer drops to the floor. It's not clear why, but he's upset about something. Chester walks over to him. I watch carefully. He doesn't touch Gus or say anything. He bends his head a little to where Gus is looking so Gus knows he's there.

Gus's hands go up to his ears, like there's too much noise, except there isn't any noise. He's agitated. Maybe he was having too much fun with Amelia.

"Looks like we shouldn't stay too much longer," Sara says. "But thank you for this, Connie. Amelia is wonderful with Gus."

It's nice of Sara to say it this way.

Sara comes into the room, picks up Gus's computer, and touches his shoulder. "C'mon, Gussie. No meltdowns here, please. Amelia and her mom want to watch you do a good job saying thank you for the visit and see you later, Amelia."

She sounds so casual in all this that I almost miss it. Did she just say meltdown? Is this a meltdown? We all hold our breath and wait. And then—the moment passes. He was making a high-pitched whining sound, but he stops when his mom touches his shoulder. He holds up one hand and repeats the last words his mom gave him. "See you later, Amelia."

No meltdown.

I'm shocked. Except for his speech, which he was reading out loud, it's more than I've heard Gus say to another child. But Chester doesn't seem surprised. Sara keeps looking at him. "And what else, Gus?"

He's not sure. He bounces a little, and then, without any prompting, he says, "Thank you for the nice visit."

I turn to Chester. "That was amazing! I can't believe it!"

"Oh sure," Chester says, following them as they start toward the front door. "That's the thing about our people. They keep changing. They get better in lots of little ways. Amelia will, too."

I catch Connie's eye and I can see she's thinking the same thing.

"Sara—" Connie says as Sara and Gus near the front door. "Can we make this a regular thing? It's good for Amelia, too. To be honest, it would be good for both of us to have more company in our lives."

Sara turns and gives Connie a hug. "Of course," she says. "We'd love it. As long as I can cancel at the last minute if Gus is having a bad day and you can, too, if you need to."

"Amelia's been having a hard time lately. This has helped a lot."

Sara knows, of course. She doesn't need Connie to say it.

"I think these kids can help each other," Sara says. "They understand certain things that you and I might not." Sara looks down at Chester and then at me. "Kind of like the pets, actually. I think they understand a lot more than we realize. I don't know, maybe that's crazy. Maybe they're just sweet animals."

CHAPTER TWENTY-SIX

FOR THE REST OF THE NIGHT, Amelia seems different. She talks more. And smiles. When Connie makes a joke, she even laughs a little.

Alone in our room, I choose my words carefully. "I think maybe you can hear me, Amelia, but it's not because there's anything wrong with you. Your brain works differently, which means you're very good at certain things and bad at other things. You're good at mental math and drawing and learning about cats. You're not good at social skills or understanding other kids. But that doesn't mean you won't ever have friends! You already do! Gus is your friend! So is Chester!"

I wait to see if there's any response. There isn't.

"And me. I'm your friend."

Amelia doesn't look at me, but she doesn't do anything

else, which I think means she's listening.

I keep going. "Here's the important part, though. You have to decide—do you want to go back to school so you can practice this friend-making business? I think maybe you do, but you're also pretty scared, which is understandable."

I stop talking because I've just remembered something Chester said: "Don't talk too much at once. Then they'll stop listening."

It's hard, though.

There's so much I want to say.

She still doesn't answer. Instead of saying anything, she draws again, starting a new page, dividing it up into panels. I jump up on the bed beside her desk. "Are you ever going to show me what you're working on?"

I put a paw on the desk. "Please? I promise I'll like it. I know some cats seem judgmental sometimes, but I won't be like that."

She puts one arm around the page so I know that she doesn't want me to look.

"Fine, I won't look until you're finished. But then I'd really like to see it."

I sit back on the bed so she knows that I mean it. I won't sneak a look.

Then she surprises me. She nods. And whispers, "I'll

show you when I'm done."

I stop the bath I was pretending to give myself. I don't want to scare her by making too much of this. Neither one of us likes big displays.

"Thanks," I say softly.

"You're welcome," she says.

I let her work quietly for a while.

Chester used to say that patience is one of the most important qualities for a service dog. Your person won't always need you and sometimes they'll have problems you can't help them with, even if you'd like to.

I should be patient, I know, but now that she's answered me, I don't want to let the chance slip away. "Do you *want* to go back to school?"

For a long time, she doesn't say anything.

"I don't know," she finally says in a voice so soft, I'm not sure if I'm hearing her or if she's just thinking it. I move up on the bed so I can watch her mouth. Yes, it's moving. "I'm scared I'll get mad and do something terrible again."

"Did you really get mad because they laughed at your shoes?"

"No."

"What did they say?"

"They did laugh about my shoes, but then Shayna asked

197

what was going on with my dad."

I'm not sure what to say to this. To me, it doesn't sound so bad. It sounds like a question old friends might ask. "Did she ask in a mean way?"

"I don't know."

"Were you mad at your dad, but instead you got mad at them?"

"I don't know. They make me mad. I can't help it."

I try this: "What I do when I get mad is I puff up my fur and walk sideways. I don't know if that helps."

She makes a sound I don't recognize. At first I'm scared she's crying again, but she's not. She's laughing.

"What's so funny?"

"Cats are funny."

"No we're not. It's a good strategy. Puffing up scares away enemies."

She's laughing harder. So hard Connie opens the door. "Is everything okay?"

Amelia nods but doesn't say anything.

She's laughing, Connie. At me. I'm not trying to be funny. I'm offering tips.

Connie smiles. Then she puts her hand over her mouth. Maybe it doesn't matter that she's laughing at me. Maybe this means I'm doing my job.

CHAPTER TWENTY-SEVEN

OVER THE NEXT COUPLE OF DAYS, I make a few mistakes.

In the beginning, I talk too much. I'm so happy to have Amelia understand me that I can't stop telling her everything I've been thinking for the last month. Admittedly, not all of it involves her. I tell her my favorite flavors of canned food. I tell her I miss going outside, even though it was scary the one time I did. I tell her my strategies for keeping myself clean.

"I can't listen to all this," Amelia finally says. She whispers now, so Connie won't know she's talking to me. "I'm trying to *concentrate*."

She's sitting at her desk working on her book.

I feel bad. Later, I apologize. "Rocky used to say I talked too much, too."

"It's okay. I just can't hear it after a while. It's like noise in my head."

I think about this. I remember Chester saying he tried not to talk too much, and only say important things. "I pick and choose," he said. "Gus hates small talk so I don't do it."

I'm not sure what "small talk" is, but I can probably guess. Chester's right. I have to think about what's most important right now. It isn't cat food flavors.

"I'd like to tell you my real name," I say after I've let her work quietly for a few hours. "It's Franklin, not Benjamin. You were very close, though. I don't know how you knew."

She turns away from her book and considers this. "I don't know either. You just looked like Benjamin Franklin to me, but I'm not sure why. Do you want me to start calling you Franklin?"

Now that she's asking, I'm suddenly not sure. I don't feel like the same cat that I was with Emily and her family. Back then I mostly cared about chasing a string around the house and batting at bugs. I'm different now.

"Franklin sounds a little like a grandpa's name," Amelia says. "Maybe we could think of a nickname."

I think about the nicknames Emily had for me and hold my breath.

"Maybe Frankie? Would that be okay?"

"Yes," I say. "That might be okay."

That evening I ask if she'd consider going back to school if she didn't have to see Maura and Shayna. I keep thinking about Rajah and the way he's allowed to choose the other animals he has to spend time with. I wonder if it's possible for Amelia to do the same thing.

"I will see them, though. They're always there."

"But what if your mom asked Ms. Pitts to put you in a different class?" I know there are two fifth-grade classes because Chester used to complain about how crowded recess got with both fifth-grade classes outside at once.

Amelia thinks for a while. "It'll just happen again. I'll try not to get so mad, but I will. It always happens. And afterward it's always my fault."

I don't say anything. I'm choosing my words carefully and I'm certainly not going to suggest puffing up and walking sideways again. I've tried that.

Later, though, I think of a different strategy. "Do you think your dad might have had this problem when he was a kid? And that's why he got kicked off his mathlete team?"

"I don't want to talk about my dad."

"Okay, but do you remember what he did?"

"I told you, I don't want to talk about it."

"Fine, but can I just say this one little thing? Do you remember what he did? How he came to the tournament and took notes anyway and then he got back on the team and they all got to be friends?" I wait for a moment and then keep going. "I think he might have had the right idea. If you feel bad about something you've done, maybe you should go back and show people that you're sorry by doing something nice."

For a long time Amelia doesn't say anything. She also doesn't work on her book. She's thinking.

Finally she says, "When I try to be nice to people, they make fun of me and laugh. It never works."

I remember the jeering faces of the other students and how quickly they changed their minds about wanting me. I got scared on Sara's shoulder, and they all turned on me. Amelia might be right.

Then I think of something else: "You were nice to Gus on his last visit. It worked with him."

"He's different."

"Why?"

"He's easier."

"I bet some kids would say he's harder to be nice to. You figured out a way."

"It's not hard with him because he hates the same things I do."

"Like what?"

"Too much talk. Too many questions. That's why we both like being quiet with Chester."

I try not to take this personally. "I don't talk *all* the time."

"You talk a *lot*."

To prove that I don't always talk too much, I don't say anything for the rest of the night.

But I'm thinking.

CHAPTER TWENTY-EIGHT

THE NEXT DAY, AN IDEA COMES to me.

I've spent most of the night trying to think of nice things Amelia might do for the other kids at school. I thought of suggesting that she make a cardboard box bedroom for all the other students, but know that would probably be hard to pull off. Then I thought of something simpler: Amelia should go back and compete in the Math Olympiad.

Even though I know she doesn't want to, I tell her she should do it anyway because they have no one who is good at mental math and besides, one of their team members is sick, so they'll be disqualified if she doesn't. "Doing something you don't want to is a way to show people that you're a really nice person. Which you are. Everyone should see that."

Naturally, Amelia doesn't like the idea at first.

"No way" is her answer.

"What if you tell them ahead of time, mental math questions only. Tell them you can't help on the other questions, and then they won't expect it. Mental math is easy for you and hard for everyone else!"

She doesn't say no again, which I take as a good sign.

"It would mean that you could look over your dad's study guide, and maybe even study a little with him. Which might also be nice."

"I don't know about that. My dad isn't good at explaining anything. He just answers the questions and expects me to figure out how he got it."

"Can you explain how you do mental math in your head?"

"No."

"Maybe he's the same way. Maybe you can ask him to slow down and explain things more."

"I don't know. Ever since he started going out with Sandy, I don't like my dad that much and he doesn't like me either."

"I think you're mad at your dad. I thought I hated Emily and her whole family when they drove away and left me outside. I must have talked about it a lot, because finally Rocky told me, I didn't hate them, I loved them, and that's why I was so mad."

For a long time, neither one of us says anything.

Finally I say, "When your dad looked through your book, he really, really liked it. So did I."

I know this is a risk—we weren't supposed to look at her book and we did. It might remind her of another reason to be mad at her dad.

"He doesn't want me to be an artist. He says artists don't make money," she says.

"It's okay not to listen to everything he says. I didn't listen to Rocky sometimes. I was right not to. You don't have to do math for the rest of your life. Just for the tournament."

"I'm pretty sure you still do math in high school."

I'm happy to hear that she's planning on going to high school.

"Fine. You'll do a little more afterward."

"What if I get something wrong and freak out?"

"I don't think you will," I say. But this reminds me of another idea. "You should invite Gus and Sara to come to the tournament. That way, Chester will be right there to help if you have any problems. He's trained for this kind of thing. I think it'll be okay and it might even be better than that. You might help them and then you'll be a hero and everyone will forget about the whole scratching Shayna thing."

"No they won't."

"You're right, maybe they won't. But they'll forgive you. Especially if you also apologize to her."

Maybe I'm going overboard here, but one look at her face and I think it's working. She's considering my idea.

Later that night, Connie says, "Good night, you two." Usually Amelia goes right to sleep and so do I. Cats might be nocturnal creatures, but we all have trouble staying awake when we're inside and nothing's going on.

"Frankie?" she says.

"Yes?"

"I think you're right. I should go back to the math team. I'm scared, though."

"Of course you are," I say. "It's okay to be scared."

CHAPTER TWENTY-NINE

"OH, SWEETHEART, THAT'S A WONDERFUL idea," Connie says the next morning when Amelia announces that she wants to go back to do the Math Olympiad. She also makes it clear that she'll go back for team practice, but she won't go to class yet; she's not ready.

An hour ago in our room, I said, "Tell her you'll be ready soon. Just not yet."

Now she says, "I'll be ready soon. Just not yet."

It's a good feeling, I have to admit. Hearing myself talk out loud.

"Of course. That's a good idea. We'll take it nice and slow. I'll call Ms. Pitts today. She'll be so excited."

It turns out that Ms. Pitts *is* happy, and so is the teacher who runs the math team. "She says you'll need to work a little to catch up with the others. They've learned some concepts that you might not know."

Connie looks at Amelia as she says this, to see how nervous this makes her.

Amelia says, "I'm not going to be able to learn all that. There isn't time. I'm going to be the person on the team who does all the mental math, but that's it. We should tell them that ahead of time."

She's doing a great job!

"Actually, you're right," Connie says. "There isn't really time for you to learn all these things. Let me explain this to her and see what she thinks."

Later Connie comes in and says she's talked to the teacher and it's okay if Amelia hasn't mastered all the subject areas. This is it! It's going to work!

Now the only thing she has left to do is take a shower.

Connie suggests she take a shower the day *before* she goes back to practice.

"It's a good idea," I say after Connie leaves the room. "This way if anything goes wrong, you have a whole day to recover." I pause. "Not that anything will go wrong."

It's hard for me to help Amelia with the shower. I can't

imagine the agony of getting in a shower. And then know-ing you'll have to repeat the whole nightmare again in a few days.

"Would it help to have Frankie in the bathroom with you?" Connie asks.

Amelia nods. She's standing in the bathroom, naked except for a towel. The way she's slouching makes her look small.

I'm happy at the nod. Though I might hate showers, I have to admit I love watching them. I can't really explain it. Water running down a shower door is more interesting to me than almost anything else. Better, even, than watching squirrels fight over a tiny acorn.

That my pleasure might come at the expense of Amelia's comfort is not something I'm proud of.

Amelia takes the fastest shower on record, possibly. It might be less than two minutes total, but she's done it. Soaped her whole body and washed her hair, too.

That's all that matters.

Without crying or screaming (just a little tiny moaning, so soft it's possible only I can hear) and that's it. She shuts the water off and steps out.

"Great job!" I say, not taking my eyes off the dripping water. "Really great!"

I don't look up at her face until I'm reasonably sure the last drop has fallen and then I see: she's wrapped in a new, fluffy towel Connie bought. Her skin is a soft, happy pink and she's looking in the mirror with a smile on her face.

She looks fine. Happy, even. And definitely proud of herself.

"This is the way Amelia has decided she will participate," Connie explains to Jack over the phone. "She doesn't want to add extra pressure on herself by trying to master new material. She'll go to the last practice before the tournament. She'll help her team as much as possible, in the best way she can. The teacher says that's fine. They're a little desperate, I guess, because one kid is sick so they wouldn't have a full team without her."

Connie is explaining all this to Jack over the phone. It sounds like he's said he doesn't want to help her study if she isn't interested in learning the material.

"You can show her the areas and possible questions where her mental math ability might be a help, even if she hasn't mastered the overall concepts."

For a long time, Connie doesn't speak and I can't hear what he says.

"Fine . . . yes, all right. Fine. We'll see you then."

It sounds like he's coming over, but what has she agreed to? I do think Amelia should at least talk to her dad and figure out how to be with him so the mere mention of his name doesn't produce meltdowns, but I'm also worried that if this goes badly, Amelia will have showered for nothing because she won't want to go to practice tomorrow.

"Hi, Am," Jack says that afternoon. He stands in the doorway but doesn't come into her room. "Your mom says you're going to math practice tomorrow."

She's sitting at her desk with her back to the door. She nods but doesn't turn around.

"That's great. I'm glad. Have you looked over my old study guide? Maybe I could walk you through some of the problems."

She *has* been looking over his study guide, but she doesn't tell him this. She has something else on her mind.

"Are you going to move in with Sandy?" she asks softly.

"We found a place a few nights ago, so yes. We'll be moving in next month."

"Does that mean we'll never go to the zoo again?"

Jack looks surprised. "Of course not. We can still go to

the zoo. Maybe we won't go with Sandy is all. I got a little annoyed when she said all that stuff about Rajah not being happy in his domain. You know him a lot better than she does."

I'm surprised to hear him say this, but it seems to make Amelia feel better. "Maybe you should break up with her."

Jack laughs as if Amelia is joking, which she isn't. "No, Am. I'm learning that it's possible to be annoyed by someone and still love them. I can be annoying to Sandy, too—believe me, she tells me—but we still love each other."

This is confusing. She doesn't like Sandy, so how can her dad say he loves her? "What about me?"

"Being with Sandy doesn't change how I feel about you."

Amelia thinks about this for a while. So do I.

Jack keeps going: "Did getting this new cat change the way you feel about Rajah?"

Amelia reaches down and pulls me into her lap. "No. I love them both."

It's the first time Amelia has ever said this. I purr so she knows I feel the same way without having to interrupt.

"There you go. I feel the same way."

I get the feeling that it's hard for Jack to talk about feelings, because he reaches for the study guide and says, "We should probably go over some problems, right?"

Maybe it's hard for Amelia, too, because she says, "Okay, sure."

And they do.

For a long time, they talk about math. It's hard for me to tell if Amelia understands what he's saying, or if she's only pretending to understand. She nods a lot and says, "Okay, I get it now."

Finally they get to the last page and he says, "I think you'll be in good shape. You know more than you think you do."

Amelia looks down. "Not really," she says softly. "The thing is, I don't really like math that much."

I'm surprised to hear her be so honest, but Jack nods. "I know," he says. "It's more my thing than yours. I was thinking that after this Olympiad business is over, maybe we should find a real art class for you. Maybe something in the extension program at my school. I told your mom and she thinks it's a good idea."

Amelia's eyebrows go up. I wish I could tell him, *That's a great idea! Good job, Jack!*

"You know, only if you want to."

"I do. I'd love to take an art class."

Jack looks around the room, as if now that he's made this nice offer, he's not sure what else to say. "Would you like to show me your book? I only got to see part of it before."

Even Connie hasn't asked to see her book. I think she assumes Amelia will say no.

"I liked what I saw. I'd love to see more."

Amelia doesn't do anything at first. I know she's considering this carefully. Her dad might say the wrong thing, or get bored before she's finished showing him. It's hard to show people something important. I don't say anything because she should make this decision herself.

Which she does. She gets up from the bed, opens her desk drawer, and pulls her book out. She sits back down on the bed, making enough space so her dad can sit next to her, with room on the other side so I can see, too.

She opens the book to the first page. "It's called *The Long, Long Adventure*," she says. "It's about a cat who gets lost from his old home and has to find a new one," she says.

"Huh," Jack says. "That sounds interesting."

"There's a lot the cat doesn't understand about the world because he's pretty young when he gets lost from his first family. He's not good at making friends with other cats. Any time he tries to, he gets into a cat fight. It makes him feel terrible, like maybe he's all alone in the world. But then he makes friends with a raccoon who teaches him about eating out of garbage cans so he's not hungry anymore and he's not friendless. The raccoon is like a dad to him for a long time, only one night the raccoon eats too much and can't move quickly and he gets hit by a car in the middle of the road. It's terrible. It's the hardest thing that's ever happened to him and it means he's on his own again."

It's hard not to feel emotional, hearing Amelia tell my whole story.

As she does, she turns the pages of the book. The pictures include a lot of details: the lawn mower in the shed, the chicken bones we found the first night. She is great at drawing details and it's easy to tell what everything is. The more she talks, the more I realize how much my life story is like her life, only her dad didn't get hit by a car, he got hit by love.

I try to imagine what it would have been like if I'd had to watch Rocky go off with a new best friend who was an opossum or something like that. It would have been hard. I would have wondered, for a long time, if there was something wrong with me.

"After that, the cat knows he needs to find a family to live with, so he goes out looking for one. At first he finds one with a dog he likes but they can't keep him because the dad is allergic, so he has to find another one. He gets really scared that maybe he won't find one because a lot of families say no."

The longer this story goes on, the more my throat tightens. Suddenly it's getting hard for me to see the pictures. It's like my eyes are clouding up or something.

I don't think Jack is feeling the same way. He's making a coughing noise like maybe this story is going on too long. It makes Amelia nervous and she shuts the book. "I haven't finished it yet. I'm not sure how it ends."

I wish I could tell her right now: *It ends with you! You're the hero of my story!* But I can't say that right now. It might distract her from this visit with her dad. And even though he might not be quite as interested in her book as I am, he's been nice, asking to see it.

"It's good," her dad says. "You're a good artist."

"Thanks," she says softly.

CHAPTER THIRTY

THE OLYMPIAD IS ONLY TWO DAYS away, which means Amelia doesn't have much time to study, but it also means she doesn't have to take another shower.

She's told me a few times that the practice went fine. If I ask for more details, she says there weren't any. "We went through a bunch of math problems. That was it, pretty much."

"They didn't wonder where you've been? Or ask you any questions?"

"Not really. They were just worried about being prepared."

"Are you?"

"I don't know. I told them I probably wasn't going to be able to help that much. One boy said, 'We know,' and another boy said, 'It's okay. We'd be disqualified for not having enough people so you've already helped us.'"

That was nice. I hope it's enough to make Amelia less nervous.

The prep sheet she brought home says boys should wear a button-down shirt and pants that aren't jeans or elastic waist. Girls should wear something "casually dressy." To Amelia, these words are confusingly vague. "Casual" and "dressy" are opposites, clothes-wise.

"Why would an organization for smart people write something stupid like this?" she asks Connie, who rolls her eyes and doesn't say anything.

Amelia plays a trick on the rules by wearing an elastic-waist skirt.

We know that Chester and Gus will be there because Sara called Connie last night and said they were excited to come and cheer Amelia on. I could tell this made Connie happy because she sat down on the sofa and put her hand on her chest.

"Thank you," she said into the phone. "I mean it. Thank you."

It's possible they've been talking more because just before they leave for the tournament, Connie comes in and says, "If you get nervous or overwhelmed, Sara says it's fine for you to borrow Chester for a few minutes. You can sit quietly with him."

At first, I admit, this worried me. Amelia is *my* person. Chester will have enough to do, keeping Gus calm in a crowded auditorium full of people talking about math problems that he doesn't understand.

"I think I should go, too, don't you?" I say to Amelia, even though I know she can't answer me now, in front of her mom. "It'll be fine. I'll stay in my carrier the whole time."

"No," Amelia says, accidentally out loud.

"No—what?" Connie says.

"Nothing. Frankie wants to come but he can't. If he does, I'll just worry about him the whole time."

Connie bends down and scratches behind my ear. "Do you wish you could come, Frankie?"

"Don't encourage him, Mom. He can't."

I can't get over how harsh Amelia sounds. I know she doesn't mean to, which is what worries me most: it's like she's already on edge, her temper fraying.

"Fine, I won't come," I say quickly. "But you need to remember to just. Stay. Calm. No scenes, please, okay?"

"OKAY," she sighs, exasperated.

✦ ✦ ✦

After they leave, I do nothing but worry. I can't sleep at all, so I walk from room to room. When a cluster of birds gathers on the same tree branch outside Amelia's window that I once spent a night on, I tap the window with my paw. "Have any of you been over at the high school this morning?" I call out. "Can you tell me what's going on over there?"

A few of them see that I'm a cat and fly away. The younger, braver ones stay and stare at me. They don't answer, of course. Birds don't care what people do apart from which ones keep their feeders full. The rest of the time, they chatter to themselves in such high, squeaky voices, the rest of us can't understand what they're saying.

But now I need their help. Amelia and Connie have been gone too long. I want to know if the tournament is still going on. Birds might not be able to tell me this, but they can fly over the school and tell me if cars are still in the parking lot.

"THE HIGH SCHOOL," I call again. "WOULD ONE OF YOU MIND FLYING OVER THERE AND SEEING IF THERE ARE STILL CARS IN THE PARKING LOT?"

They cock their heads and look around blank-faced. This is the whole problem with birds. They have all the freedom in the world, and they don't do anything with it.

The sky is dark when they finally get home. I can guess before they even walk inside that it hasn't gone well. Before they left, Connie said they might invite Gus and Chester over for ice cream afterward to celebrate if it went well.

There's no sign of Gus or Chester, which is my first clue.

Also, they're walking far apart, not talking. Amelia's arms are folded across her chest.

When they get inside, Connie uses a tone that I now think of as her fake-cheerful voice. She's used it in the past when Amelia's gotten in trouble and she's tried to pretend it's not that big of a deal, even though it is. "Hello, kitty," Connie says to me. "You must be hungry. You haven't had your dinner yet. Will you feed him, Am?"

Amelia doesn't answer or make a move toward my bowl. Her face is blank in a way that scares me. I don't care about my dinner.

"How did it go?" I ask her.

She won't look at me or say anything. My heart speeds up.

"Just tell me, was it bad? Nod once if it was bad."

Nothing.

"Was Chester there? Did he help you?"

Nothing.

I have to wait until we're alone in our room, but when we are, she still won't talk. Something terrible must have happened, because she doesn't do any of her usual things. She doesn't bounce or rock. She doesn't flip through her notebook. She sits down on her bed and stares ahead, blankly.

"Whatever happened, this wasn't your fault," I say. "If anything, it's my fault. I suggested this even though I don't know anything about Math Olympiads. It was probably too stressful. It was a terrible idea."

I hear Connie's voice on the phone in the other room. It's louder and higher than I expected, almost like she's laughing, but how can that be? Something terrible has happened and Connie's *laughing*?

I move out into the hall to hear her better.

"I know, I couldn't believe it either. It went on for *hours*. As other teams got eliminated they were allowed to leave and I was getting so tired I actually started hoping that would happen to us. But we hung in there. Finally it was down to two teams and, I couldn't believe it. We won!"

What?

They won? How is that possible?

If they won, what's happened to Amelia?

The next morning, Amelia seems better, at least enough to tell me the story of what happened at the tournament. At first she was fine and was even able to help her teammates, but after a few hours, the questions got harder and more theoretical. She started to get frustrated. Then the other teams kept asking for questions to be repeated so they could have more time, and she wanted to scream.

"They kept asking, even after they'd heard the question three times. It was like they were cheating, and it was making me so, so mad."

Instead of getting mad, though, she asked for permission to use the bathroom. "The problem was there's a lot of rules around going to the bathroom. If you leave, you have to wait for the next question before you can come back. They don't want anyone cheating by using a calculator, I guess."

So she waited in her toilet stall. And waited some more. She kept expecting someone to come tell her it was time to return, but no one did. After a while, she got worried. With all the crazy rules they had, maybe she had stayed away too long and had gotten her whole team disqualified. The moment she had that thought, she assumed it was true. She had no idea how long she'd been in the bathroom, but it might have been close to a half hour.

She started to cry because she assumed she'd lost the tournament for her team and everyone was so mad, they left without saying anything to her.

That was when her dad came in and asked if everything was okay. "No," she said. Her face was red from crying. "I can't go back now. I don't know what happened."

"Nothing happened," her dad said. "They're still playing."

That's when he told her he'd talked to one of the judges, who said they wouldn't disqualify the team if Amelia was feeling sick and had to leave.

Suddenly she felt embarrassed more than anything else. Partly because her dad had gone to the trouble of talking to the judge and partly because he was standing in the girls' bathroom.

"You shouldn't be in here, Dad," she told him.

"Right," he said. "So what do you think? Do you want to come back and finish the tournament or do you want to go home now? It doesn't matter to me. You might feel better if you come back and then when it's over, you can pretend you had a great time. We'll know the truth, but other people won't."

She couldn't get over her dad saying, *We'll know the truth.*

She'd been pretending a lot lately—that she liked playing the same games at recess as the other kids, that she cared about the same things Maura and Shayna did. You had to pretend if you didn't want to spend all of recess alone, but lately, she'd started to think that pretending was too hard and she couldn't do it anymore.

But her dad's words made her feel better. She paused for a moment as she told me this story. Finally she shrugged. "I don't know. Like maybe he understands more than I thought he did." She bends down and gives my ears a scratch. I close my eyes so she knows I'm both listening and enjoying the ear rub.

She pulls me into her lap for the rest of the story. In the end, she went back and finished up the tournament. It was nice to win, but she didn't feel like she had that much to do with it. She'd only helped with about four questions in the beginning. It wasn't her victory. So what was the point?

She still won't have anyone to talk to at recess or eat lunch with in the cafeteria. Her teammates aren't in the same grade as her, so she couldn't eat with them even if they asked her to, which they probably never would.

"It doesn't really change anything," she sighs. "I still won't have anyone to talk to at school."

I think I understand the problem. I remember this feeling from living on my own after Rocky died. I started wandering around more, down unfamiliar streets, meeting animals I'd never seen before. One night I saw a fox chase after a cat who was smaller than me. Another morning I watched a brown bear lumber up the street. I survived both brushes with danger, which was a relief, but afterward made me sadder than before because I had no one to share these stories with.

Suddenly I understood why mice chattered endlessly just before their end. Feeling all these emotions is hard. You want to share them. You need to tell someone.

The day after I saw the bear, I sat out in the open on the woodpile in Gus's backyard for the first time. I needed a home for food, of course, but I needed more than that. I needed a family to share my stories with.

When I looked in the windows, I saw one boy alone, staring back at me. We watched each other for a long time, or at least I thought we did. *He could be a friend*, I let myself think.

I didn't know him then. I didn't realize he already had a best friend in Chester. But feeling all this got me ready to watch Chester in action and find my own best friend.

Which I have.

I tell Amelia, "Maybe it's okay if you don't make new friends right away at school. Gus and Chester will always be there. Plus you've got me at home. And your mom and dad. None of us are perfect, but that isn't too bad."

"I don't know," she says. "Maybe."

❧ ❧ ❧

Later that morning, there's a surprise: Sara, Chester, and Gus come over with doughnuts and juice to celebrate the victory. They left the tournament early, so they want to hear how the second half went. As Connie tells Sara and Gus one version, I tell Chester another. "Amelia got tired and frustrated. She almost had a meltdown and wanted to accuse the other team of cheating, but then she didn't. Instead, she went to the bathroom, cooled off for a while, and came back."

Telling the story this way, I realize, makes it a better story.

"Oh, that's great to hear," Chester says. "She should be very proud of herself."

"She is. But she's also worried it won't change anything at school. Maura and Shayna won't care that her math team won."

"No, that's true. They probably won't."

"They'll still make her feel bad if she tries to eat lunch with them. Or they'll make all their mean suggestions if she plays with them at recess."

"They might."

We stop talking for a while and watch the others eat their doughnuts and drink their cider. Amelia invites Gus to sit next to her on the sofa so they can play with his talking board. It's easy to see that being with Gus is good for Amelia. She knows that playing with the sound effects will make them both laugh for a while, but they shouldn't do it for too long because the pets don't like it and after a while, Gus's ears hurt, too.

Having this friend takes her mind off other worries.

"I do have one idea. I don't know if Amelia will be interested, but maybe you could ask her."

I love Chester's ideas, but I don't want to sound too eager, like I can't think of any ideas myself, even though the truth is, I can't. "What is it?" I say.

"Maybe Amelia could eat lunch with me and Gus. Ms. Pitts has been trying something new where she assigns a different peer to sit with us so he can practice asking other kids questions. It's worked surprisingly well so far. Everyone loves Ms. Pitts so a lot of kids signed up to take turns. Even Maura and Shayna are on the list."

They are? I'm shocked! "Don't they want to sit with their own friends?"

"There are so many names that each person only does it once every few weeks. I might have thought they'd get bored with it, but it turns out kids like to help. They just need to be showed how to do it. Ms. Pitts gives them both a list of questions to ask each other. About favorite hobbies and TV shows. Gus has some of his answers preprogrammed on his computer, so that makes it easier. And he's getting better. Sometimes he comes up with a new question and types it in. That's always a nice surprise."

It *is* a nice surprise. Chester is right. They both keep changing and getting better, bit by bit.

"It's a good idea, Chester, but it only takes care of one lunch every few weeks if all the other kids are doing it, right?"

"Not necessarily. Just the other day, I heard Ms. Pitts say that she wanted to find another student who could eat with Gus and his lunch partner every day so she could fade away the teacher aide who usually sits with them."

"So she could do it every day?"

"If she likes it."

This could give her a chance to get to know other kids, too. Amelia would like that. I know she would. I think of something else. "Have you ever heard about a lunch group that Ms. Pitts runs, where kids eat in her office and work on social skills?"

"Yes. Gus tried it a few times, but it was too hard for him. He'll try again at some point."

"Do you think it would be good for Amelia?"

"Definitely. There were two other girls in it. They're

fourth graders, I think, but she might like them."

It's funny, I realize. An hour ago, I thought Amelia was right, that nothing would change if she went back to school. Now I'm thinking differently.

On the sofa, Gus starts to rock, like maybe he's getting bored with the game he's playing with Amelia. Sara stops talking and looks over.

I watch Sara's face. I see her almost say something and then she stops herself, because Amelia is typing on Gus's computer. She waits to see what Amelia's message says.

Amelia presses a button and the machine speaks. "I have an idea, Gus. Would you like to take our animals outside? We can show you the tree that Frankie tried to climb and then got stuck in." The voice sounds like the one Gus has picked for himself—a man with a British accent.

Chester looks at me. "How about that?" he says. He looks like he's smiling, though of course a dog panting to go outside always looks like he's smiling.

I line up behind him as Amelia stands up.

"Is this okay, Mom? Can we take Chester and Frankie outside?"

Connie considers this for a moment, then smiles and nods. "Sure. For a little while."

It's a beautiful day; no one needs a jacket or a hat. Sara puts a leash on Chester, though of course he doesn't need one. It's only to let the neighbors know that he won't do anything unexpected.

Amelia picks me up and tucks me partway under the sweater she's wearing. I'm too big to fit, but if anyone sees us, it's possible I'll look like a purse or a grocery bag. "I'll put you down when we get to the back," she whispers.

"That's fine," I say.

A moment later, Connie opens the door and we all head outside.

Keep reading for a sneak peek at *Chester and Gus!*

How to Tell Time

I'VE LIVED IN MY NEW HOME for three days but I still haven't met the boy I'm supposed to be best friends with.

He's nervous, I think.

So am I.

I don't know very many boys. I played with one once in the park where Penny brought me so I could get used to little children pulling on my fur and grabbing my tail. The boy in the park threw a ball and then a stick for me to fetch. When he got tired of that game, he said he was going to show me something called a slide that would be the most fun thing I'd ever done in my whole life. He picked me up and carried me to the top of it.

It was *not* fun. It was the opposite of fun. It was the most scared I've ever been except for the first time Penny practiced the "Dog Left Alone" test and tied me to a post for two minutes while she walked away. Afterward, she told me I wasn't supposed to whine or bark or show any signs of anxiety, which I didn't know at the time because I whined and barked like crazy. I couldn't help it. I was so anxious. This is what happens when you're a puppy. Your brain is so busy, you lose track of someone for a second and you think, *I haven't seen her for hours. She's probably dead.* You don't even know what dead is and you think it.

It's embarrassing now when I look back on it. I got nervous over lots of things back in those days.

When Penny came back, I dribbled pee I was so relieved to see her again! She knelt down and said, "It's okay, Chester. I was only gone two minutes," and I thought, *Really? Was it only two minutes? It felt more like two hours.*

I've never had a great sense of time and back then I wasn't completely sure what those words meant. Now I know. Two minutes is about the same as in a sec, and an hour means dinner's not for a long, long time, possibly days.

I loved our time at the park until that day the big boy carried me to the top of a slide and pushed me down. After that, I didn't love our trips to the park anymore.

Work

I KNOW I SHOULDN'T COMPLAIN ABOUT MY new home or this boy I haven't seen yet. It's my fault that I'm here, living with people who don't know their son very well if they got him a dog that he doesn't want to meet.

I was meant to be a service dog like my mother. She was a guide dog for a blind man until she got hit by a car, and then she retired to be a mother. "Being a mother is an important job, too," she told us, but she didn't really mean it. Having puppies made her tired and not very happy. Thinking about her old job made her happy.

"There's no better feeling than knowing there's one person in the world who depends entirely on you," she told us once. We were still small then and lying in a heap on top

3

of each other. I had my brother Hershey's ear in my mouth. We all stopped what we were doing and listened.

"You meet your person and you *connect*. You learn what that person needs and you do it for them. It's the most satisfying feeling in the world."

After that we tried harder to pay attention during our puppy trainings. My sister Cocoa asked every person who gave us kibble or a drink of water, "Are you my person? Are *you*?"

Cocoa wasn't the smartest puppy in our litter. She was always eating things she wasn't supposed to.

One morning after breakfast, I looked up and saw a big group of people walking up the driveway of our farm. A few of them rolled in wheelchairs. One wore dark glasses.

Our people! I thought. *There they are!*

I ran to Cocoa and told her to come quick and look, but she was trying to eat a pinecone and didn't want to. My brother Hershey walked with me to the edge of our play yard and watched the group for a while.

Finally he said, "I want the big man in the rolling chair with pictures on his arms. You can have any of the others."

My heart started to beat faster. I didn't know how this worked—if we got to pick them or if they picked us. "Do we know enough yet to be paired with our person?" I asked.

"Yes," Hershey said. He was the biggest in our litter and

4

acted like he knew everything. "This is how it goes. Tomorrow we'll start our jobs. Remember, the man with pictures on his arms is mine."

For the rest of the morning, I worried. I thought about our mother's stories of her life with the blind man. *I did everything for Donald. I opened doors, I pressed elevator buttons, I guided him through traffic. Yes, I got hit by a car, but the important thing is: He didn't.*

There was so much I didn't understand. What was an elevator? What was traffic?

In the afternoon, we watched the people come outside with a group of dogs who were all wearing blue vests on their backs. Our mother came over to watch with us. When we pestered her with questions—*What are they wearing? What are they doing?*—she told us to be quiet.

"Just watch," she said. "This is the most important afternoon of their lives. They're being chosen by their person."

For the next hour, we watched them do tricks.

"Beautiful," our mother whispered under her breath. "Just beautiful."

"Sheesh," my brother Milton said softly. "That doesn't look like much fun."

"Fun isn't the point," Hershey snapped. "The point is getting someone to choose us."

I looked over at Hershey—his ears set forward, his nose working, taking it all in. I knew what he was thinking: *I want to wear a blue vest. I want to be chosen.*

I felt it too. We all did.

After the group went inside, we asked our mother more questions. "Learning all that will be the hardest thing you've ever done. You'll live with a trainer for almost a year and work constantly. That's all I can tell you. Even after all that work, some of you won't make it. That's just how it is."

She turned around and went back to her bed. That was that.

None of us knew what to think. Cocoa couldn't stop crying. "I don't want to *work hard*. I don't want to leave our play yard."

Milton was nervous, too. "What if we can't learn all those things?" By the end of the demonstration, the dogs were doing amazing things—finding and picking up tiny objects in the grass, holding a cane steady for someone who'd dropped it. "What if we can only learn about half those tricks?"

Hershey quieted him. "This is what we were born to do. It's our calling."

Cocoa whined some more.

"Don't be a crybaby," Hershey snapped.

In the middle of the night, I woke up and realized Cocoa was missing from our pile. I got the others up to help me look. We found her at the far end of our yard, lying on her side and moaning in pain, too sick to stand up. After Wendy, from the farmhouse, wrapped her up in a blanket and took her to the vet, our mother explained, "She ate three rocks last night. I have no idea why."

For a week we didn't see Cocoa, but we learned what the word "surgery" meant when Wendy told one of the workers: "Two hours of surgery. She had to have her stomach cut open and the rocks taken out."

When she finally came back, Cocoa seemed like a different dog—not really a puppy anymore.

A week later, she was given away.

"It's okay," our mother said, after she was gone. "Some dogs aren't cut out for the working life." She sounded as if we should all just forget about Cocoa for now.

I didn't of course. How could I?

Meeting Penny

HERSHEY WAS THE FIRST ONE TO be picked by a trainer and leave the farm. He didn't even look back as he got into the man's car. It was like he'd already forgotten his dog family, he was so ready to move on to the working part of his life.

After that, each of my brothers and sisters left one by one. I asked my mother if I should be worried that no trainer had picked me yet. "I don't know," she said. "Probably."

She wasn't a big one for reassuring her puppies. She didn't see the point. "Some of you won't make it as working dogs. That's all there is to it."

She didn't say Cocoa's name, but I thought of her of course.

After the last of my littermates was taken away and it

was just the two of us, my mother said, "They might think you're too much of a worrier." She snapped at a fly and went over for some water. "Try not to act so nervous the next time a trainer comes."

A few days later, I had my chance. Penny walked into our yard and right over to me. She wore a funny green hat and shoes with plastic flowers attached to them. "Look at you!" she said, reaching out to pick me up. "They must have saved the best for last!"

I wriggled and squealed and acted like a puppy again. I was so happy to be chosen I almost left without saying goodbye to my mother. At the last minute, I went over to the bed where she slept by herself now. "I have my trainer!" I said. "I'll see you in eight months! I'll work hard, you'll see! I'll try not to be too nervous, I promise!"

She confused me then, waking up from her nap, blinking at the light. "All right," she said. "I suppose it's too late now for anything else."

In the car, Penny told me all about herself. "Dogs are my true love, Chester. That's the first thing you should know about me. I've got no husband and no kids. Just a lot of wonderful dogs who I love and train and then I take them back to the farm to be matched with their person."

At her house, she showed me pictures of the dogs from her past in frames around her living room. Some of them looked like me in other colors, like yellow and black. "I've never had a chocolate lab like you. I think that's going to make you a little different from the rest."

She smiled as she said it and pulled me into her lap. I'd known her only a few hours and already she was nicer than my mother had ever been.

How to Be Understood

"EVERY DOG HAS A WEAKNESS," PENNY told me a few weeks into my training. "They're perfect in many ways and then suddenly, they see a rabbit in the woods and all their training goes out the window. Poof, off they go. If it's not a rabbit, it'll be something else. The trick is to figure out your challenge as early as possible, then work on it *a lot*. I've got a shelf full of windup squirrels if we need them."

I loved the way Penny talked to me all the time. I always answered, hoping she would understand me. *No thanks,* I tried to tell her that time. *I don't think squirrels will be my problem. I've seen lots of squirrels. I know not to chase them.*

I thought of what my mother had said and I wanted to be

honest with Penny. I looked her in the eyes. *I'm a little anxious sometimes. It might be a problem.*

She looked back at me and smiled reassuringly. "It's okay," she said, and for a second, I thought: *She understands! She knows what I'm saying!* Then she stood up. "I'm going to get one of those squirrels right now and try it on you."

A few days later, we discovered my weakness. After the boy carried me to the top of the slide. Penny worried that I might get scared of children, so she brought me to a school one morning and we sat outside the front door, saying hello to all the students as they walked in.

I was fine! Children were sweet! One girl lifted my ear and whispered, "You're the cutest dog in the whole world." Another girl lifted my other ear and said, "I love you!"

I love you too! I tried to say, but she didn't understand.

"No yipping, Chester," Penny said firmly, with a flat hand on my nose. It didn't hurt but still, I felt embarrassed. I had to remember that I understood what people said, but they couldn't understand me. I went back to the girls and licked their hands.

That's when it happened.

A terrible sound ripped through the air. My legs went jittery and frantic. I scrambled to get under a bench. *The sky is falling! The earth is blowing up!* I screamed to Penny, but she didn't hear me. How could she with all that noise?

When the noise finally stopped, I peeked out from the bench I was hiding under. I couldn't believe it. The children weren't scared at all! They even moved toward the door where the sound had come from.

After they were gone, Penny walked over to my hiding spot and crouched down. "That was just a school bell, silly dog. It looks like maybe loud sounds might be a problem, doesn't it?"

She talked softly to me the whole drive home. She told me it would be okay, that noises might hurt my ears but they couldn't hurt my body. She let me ride in the front seat next to her again, where she could keep a hand on my back. I was still having trouble catching my breath.

Her hand felt nice. So did her voice.

"We'll practice, that's all. When you don't expect it, I'll bang a few pots and pans and you'll get used to it. Caramel had this problem, too—you remember I told you about her? She got over it eventually."

That night while I ate my dinner, Penny dropped a cookie sheet on the floor. I thought it was a bolt of lightning hitting the house. I flew out of the room and under the sofa.

"Oh dear," Penny said from the kitchen. "Looks like we've got some work to do, Chester."

After that, we worked on it all the time. Along with heeling and fetching and opening doors, Penny and I practiced loud sounds. She whistled. She set off timers. Once, she deliberately set off her smoke alarm. She even warned me ahead of time as she held the match under the alarm. "This is going to be loud, sweetheart."

It was and I panicked. I knew I wasn't supposed to. Penny had told me many times: "When a loud sound comes, sit down and wait. Don't hide. Breathe in and out until it passes. Your person will need you. They have to be able to find you when it's over."

I knew all this and I still panicked. I couldn't help it. I ran as fast as I could and got under the closest bed or table I could find.

Except for this problem, my training went well. Almost every day, Penny told me how smart I was. One time, I knew what to do for a trick before she'd even taught me. The trick was opening a drawer and getting out a pot holder. It wasn't hard. I'd watched a dog do it on a DVD, but Penny must have forgotten, because after I brought it to her she said, "You might just be the smartest dog I've ever had."

After that, she did experiments to test my "vocabulary."

She put different objects around the room and asked me to fetch one without pointing at what she wanted.

"Please bring me my car keys, Chester," she'd say, and I could. That was easy because Penny misplaced them so much. Whenever she found them, she said, "I hate you, car keys! You always walk away!" I learned the word for "shoes" the same way and also "cell phone." Once she started those tests, I worked harder to remember the names of things because it made her so happy when I did.

It didn't seem like that much of an accomplishment to me until I heard Penny on the telephone with Wendy from the farm. "I've never seen such a young dog with such a big vocabulary. There are about fifty words that he's picked up entirely on his own. And it's not just that. He's six months old and he's already got so many commands down—heel, sit-stay, crate, go now, and don't touch."

Listening to Penny made me feel good.

"I've never seen a dog like this," she said. "He's remarkable, really. There's only one weak spot, I'd say. He seems to have a bit of sound sensitivity."

Those two words weren't in my vocabulary back then, but now they are.

Don't miss *Just My Luck* by
Cammie McGovern!

Everyone has bad days.
You have to make the good ones.

JUST my LUCK

Cammie McGovern

HARPER
An Imprint of HarperCollinsPublishers

harpercollinschildrens.com